For Margaret and Arthur

'You gave me a piece of music. I heard it'
Bette Hall

Ann Sharples

Copyright Ann Sharples 2013

All rights reserved: no part of this publication
may be reproduced or transmitted by any means, electronic,
mechanical, photocopying or otherwise, without the prior
permission of the author.

This book first published in 2014
Ann Sharples

'Snowflake Symphony', text, & cover illustrations
Copyright © 2013 Ann Sharples

ISBN 978 15 007 8693 9

Ann Sharples has asserted her moral rights

www.annsharples.com

Thanks

*My thanks for help with obtaining
permissions and for their encouragement:*

*Andrew Duhon (singer/songwriter), Shan Gao, Australia, Shan
Gao, U.S.A (for locating Shan Gao in Australia for me), Baruch
Garcia, Neil Philips, Nicola Trayler-Barbrook, Chus Visor*

*My gratitude, as always, to my editor Karen Davies,
to my technician Jamie Wilson
and to my out readers Rosie Swinney and Bette Hall.*

The characters herein are entirely fictitious and in no way related to any known person.

Ann Sharples

SNOWFLAKE SYMPHONY

'Maybe the path to truth is always devious in order that surprise can hide at the turn waiting for persevering seekers'

Shan Gao

Chapter One

Spindel

My name is Spindel – or it could be Sentinel.

In one time, I experienced radius; double radius. It sliced and as it sliced, I parted; two personae out of one – to become one later, in a different place.

I was here and I was there at the same time; in both places at once .... and it began to happen. It. I cannot tell what 'it' is – not yet – perhaps further on – maybe not at all.

'In the great scheme of things' is often said. I suppose that is where I am, but not in an exact space; not in an exact time.

Gazing above and around, from my far flung position, I

hesitate. I see created, glass palaces breaking in upon the midnight sky. Drifting in through its vicinity, I cast my gaze upon the stars, a galaxy beyond, and back towards this strange city of glass; reflections of itself; a puzzle – what is actual and what a mirage; one palace reflected, or many palaces.

I pause; float towards the city, to discover what purpose it serves other than a sheer study in reflection.

My feet glide noiselessly over the surface of the streets; the silence intense. Resting, I note the intensity of silence, the significance of a pause – a space in time devoid of sound. I collect the memory; store it. In this time, in this space, I have no prediction of the future of this memory.

Reflected within this city am I, Spindel, multifaceted; each reflection as transient as myself. I am repeated as are bars of music; a chorus. Am I the music or the composer? Am I one and the same? I reflect upon this as I am reflected, thin as ice, in this glass.

I, Spindel, am a composer. I am searching for a symphony. In my mind it is a precious thing, perfect, unique. But it is not yet formed and so is an embryo, a nucleus, a speck.

My journey is as a discoverer, both as Spindel and 'mind of Spindel'; sometime Sentinel, although not now, not in this instance of resting.

As a younger, smaller being I could feel the rhythm of my environment. It made me call out in delight with its tiny, hardly discernible nuances, doubling, tripling upon itself. It lulled me to sleep and lent me a sense of security. I rode its rhythm each day, becoming disturbed if the rhythm was interrupted, lost itself .... and reassured as it returned to the beat that is its essence.

Others rode the rhythm, tussled with it, pushed against it; some let it carry them through. I, Spindel, lived the rhythm, absorbed its perfection, discarded its imperfections. And so I made my way, discovered a path to follow, revelling at each twist, turn, emboldened as I skated long, smooth straights. As I travelled I developed, honing my senses, strengthening my being.

For sustenance, I sought fragrance of taste, sweet on the lips; texture that pleased, rolling softly or riding roughly over the tongue; this from flora along the way.

I soaked in the warmth of each day, to its noon zenith and beyond, was soothed by the cool balm of evening. There are two parts to every day; one day with two contrasting parts. Each day similar in pattern .... until the path arrived at a divide as I passed round the curve of a bend.

Silence.
The rhythm paused. My heart a solitary beat with no sound.

I curled at the junction, as a foetus, on the ground, solid, a ball; metamorphosing to a steel thin disc, glinting, hovering just a small space up from the ground, settling to lie in disc form on the path.

The sudden appearance of an insistent radial arm, with a hand tense in the act of gripping a blade poised to slice, transfixed me. And slice it did, pinning my discoid self dead centre, slicing once from centre to circumference; my radius. The arm returned the blade to its pivotal position to slice an opposite radius; a cut direct and sure to complete my dissection, forming two parts. I, parted from myself, now two selves – geminal.

On that day, at that moment, I became two personae. I am Spindel, Sentinel my alter image. My form evolved diaphanous, film-like; light shimmered as it caught my skin. Sentinel emerged pushing, as does a chestnut bud about to sprout a magnificent leaf, strong, flexible, opaque; durable, sensitive, at one with the natural world and with an inner beauty of his own.

And so we were, neither acknowledging the presence of the other, but in the knowledge of being two personae; two beings before two paths.

The blade wielding arm had disappeared; no glint, no swish, no grinding point.

Peace.

Choice lay both at our feet and in our minds. We remained motionless. And then came the call; I heard it from the left branch of the path. My mind and ears strained. My feet danced – a skip, a leap; I followed the call.

Moving with time, I progressed not in leaps and bounds as my feet desired but in soft pulses, light streaming, deflecting my vision. The only way forward was to abandon myself to the pulse, allow myself to be carried through the stream of light against which the pulse, with its call, led. That call came to me as soft brush-strokes of movement gently beating a surface, creating rhythm, enticing me onwards. I became distant to myself, as a watching figure disappearing from view.

Chapter Two

Sentinel

In his room, banished there, Sentinel hears the murmur of voices below, the repetitive sounds of the progression of a household day. He stands as if abandoned.

"I am only sent away," he tells himself and stares at the scudding clouds crossing the bright blue view of sky captured by the window; his window, for it is his room.

"It is my room," he reflects and feels immediately more settled. The loneliness of being ignored settles. He is in his own time, his own space. He thinks of the woodlice living in the garden log and wonders what they are doing. To him, they are friends in whom to confide. Their confidences are amongst themselves as they are many. Sentinel has no other willing to listen.

He had made a haven in the garden, from old wire netting and covered it with pieces of wind blown branches that he laid against it. For the roof, he pressed damp moss and leaves. Inside was where he could be still and take in bird song, movement of insects, the perfume of plants. Sentinel built it one morning, labouring hard, whilst his mother was unaware, engrossed in a task of her own. When it was done, a whole creation, he felt a sense of achievement.

"Look! Look!" he exclaimed running.

"What now!"

His mother looked, her keen eyes assessing his work.

"It can stay for now," she conceded, her own task still fresh in her mind.

Sentinel experienced hope, a delight, and crawled into his small space to become a part of the garden.

Time passed.

It was with reluctance that, when summoned to eat, he crawled out and assumed his indoor self, piece by piece, as he walked obediently to the house.

There was opportunity, during the afternoon, to return, to revel in the doings and thoughts of a 'garden person'.

"Tomorrow," he thought, "tomorrow …."

Tomorrow is this day, the day of abandonment.

The evening before, he extracted what he believed to be a promise that he could play there again tomorrow before, clad in warm pyjamas, he ran up to his room and jumped happily into bed.

As sleep lulled his senses, he heard discussion, heard the door of the shed creak. Alert, he crawled to the end of his bed, which lay along the window wall, and peeped tentatively down to the garden. He watched them, with defiant stride and purposeful implements of destruction, advance to his haven. It took only moments to destroy what had taken more than an hour to create.

"No! No – no!" screamed Sentinel, standing on his bed, beating the window pane.

They started, looked up; ignored his plea and continued to drag away branches, sweep up moss and leaves.

Screaming, sobbing, distraught, Sentinel raged on; eventually exhausted by his protest he found a heavy, tear-stained sleep.

And today (which was to have been tomorrow) his room is his haven; a lonely haven which seems to float apart from the world, the world in which all else continues.

Now, staring down at the frayed carpet, relegated to his room to make way for a new carpet downstairs, he sees fields within the pattern and is inspired. Searching his box of bits and his 'toy drawer', he pulls out boxes and cartons, fencing, farm animals. With a struggle (the scissors are small and blunt) he cuts doorways and windows; here is the farmhouse, a barn, a pig sty. A mirror becomes a pond for ducks and geese.

It is done. Sentinel begins to farm.

It is a school day, soon after, with a cold, bitter wind; the bright sun a distant warmth. Sentinel; his own name for himself, a private name; hugs his scarf to his neck and runs, pounding concrete slabs of pavement, dashing across bleak roads acting as channels for the wind. On, on until the street and then the house are in view. He slows, gathers breath, anticipates the warmth indoors and allows his mind to focus on the farm upstairs. Rings the doorbell, stamps his feet.

"Don't bring that cold in here! Shut the door!"

Obedient, he complies, takes off his shoes, hangs up his outdoor clothes. Nothing to eat yet. It is too soon and the constant radio drones a daily serial. Quietly, Sentinel treads the stairs to his room; to interrupt the serial is not permitted.

No heat here. He blows on his hands. His imagination will warm him.

The farm is gone.

His head buried in the pillow, feet beneath the eiderdown, Sentinel concentrates his mind – away from desolation – on the functional, a jam sandwich and a mug of tea, later.

Over time, over childhood years, Sentinel taught himself to draw, to work out on paper what appeared in his mind. He felt as if he was primitive man in his attempts to leave his mark. In this manner, he could communicate with himself when he found it impossible to communicate with others; could hide from the terror of the world, secured by steady, grey shading, by a strong pencil line that anchored him to the page.

A balance.

'… the spin of a particle is always definite along one direction (though the spin state can always be decomposed into eigenstates of spin along another direction) …'

Shan Gao

Chapter Three

Spindel

In some instances, I spun to gaze at Sentinel; saw him engrossed with line and pattern upon paper, sometime on canvas. I slid along those curves, zigzagged jagged lines, rolled circles; turned them to spheres and revolved at speeds where line and sound became music; music at that time, in that space, too elusive to capture in my mind's eye as a score on which to work, too fleeting to retain as notes and bars.

My path is lonely, in parts will become terrifying but, even now, in this time and in this space, I can draw solace; at one with the mind that I am.

Do I mourn my alter persona? Yes; I cannot be a complete being as I am. No; Sentinel a burden restricting, holding back freedom to transcend universes, to explore without limit, because, although apart, we are inextricably attached.

It is a dark, bleak winter for Sentinel and for me, Spindel. This I realise as I reflect within the city of glass palaces. This is where I am in time and space; it is winter for Sentinel in his time and space, more earthbound than my own.

I freeze each reflected image of myself as a repetitive pattern, perhaps a chorus, and store them in my mind. I could be tens, could be thousands and more of myself. Would we travel on together as a legion, an army, or would each deflect differently and move away from its fellow, into unknown ways?

This is an abstraction, I tell myself and laugh at my mind pursuing this thread, but I may come to use it in the future.

Rested, I allow the city of glass palaces to mist over, the stars to fade, the night to grey out and dawn light to appear. With that light comes a shaft, a sunbeam to dance before me; to lure, to dazzle, to warm my being. I stretch my mind and respond, rising in its glow, gliding gilt-edged towards the direct light that the beam transmits. I step aboard the experience. It is both sound and light, light transformed into the sound of xylophones scaling upwards, more sheer upon passing through each octuple height; a run of scales lifting to a new phrase. Bars of musical light, intrinsic, sweet in tone, carry my thought; this is a part of the composition.

I know this and slide back, to be transported a second time up the scales. Yes, this phrase will repeat. It is exhilaration in ascension.

Shadow; a darkness eclipses the sun. I plummet – the exact word as the sunbeam is annihilated and the wisp of my form does not float, is pulled by gravity. There is no end to this darkness; it is forever. So it seems, but I pass ledges; the possibility of hope.

This darkness falls between the cliffs' sheer grey matter. The ledges appear flimsy. I attempt to reach out but momentum is too great a force, the void vast. I tire. This is my infinity. No. The symphony must be created. I try. Three ledges pass ... and then I grasp a moss. It tears but remains attached. I dangle, scramble, sink into the damp of the moss.

Notes cascade in discord, as if shattered glass. Their descent pierces my brain. I cannot move. I stay. I am trapped in the void, but no longer endlessly falling into oblivion.

And the phrase is captured; stored; hurts.

A new day will come.

Chapter Four

Sentinel

There was a time during childhood when Sentinel fell ill. His bed, his refuge from the world's exhaustive demands, became a furnace in which he lay, trapped. The fever rose, his brain and body burned with incessant heat no water could quench. The room pulsed as a raw heart; the walls moved from perspective to perspective, angular, surreal in proportion. A fire appeared in the grate, flames licking; burning tongues with a desire to consume. The fire a hallucination, perhaps; cinematic projection of his burning pain. It reached a peak on which Sentinel felt his whole being balance; to tip back would be unsustainable. He fell into a heavy, perspiring sleep.

Hours later, he woke to a level of calm. Both his room and his body numb, recovering from the experience. Neutral light diffused shadow. The room remained bland, unnoticeable, and Sentinel lay unfeeling, unthinking, as if frozen in time; a clock waiting to be rewound. So passed a safe day.

There were two more safe days before Sentinel had to brace himself to rejoin the world. Perhaps it would be different, perhaps a gentler place free of yawning chasms waiting for him to lose balance, to topple. Perhaps he would acquire more understanding of its needs, be able to approach life less warily. There was always 'perhaps' but, for the most part, 'perhaps' did not arrive.

Years later, as Sentinel studied, his thoughts jammed, choked on themselves. He became wedged in a cleft; a cold, desolate place where hope should have aspired.

"Everything is so restrictive", he thought. "I cannot play out my ideas, fit them into a norm. They are beyond the edge."

He could not fathom where the edge was. If he had known, perhaps he could have reined in those thoughts, ideas; perhaps not.

And so he despaired.

"Do I stay or do I leave?"

These questions accompanied his everyday, compounded.

The molten caverns of his childhood illness reappeared in the grate, conjured as they had been at that time; vivid. Sentinel grasped at paper lying close by on the floor, where he sat. He drew the fiery caverns forward, into his mind's eye, took pencils and drew; the gases combined with light, wondrous white-hot forms, flickering tongues of fire.

The sheer concentration reached a point which pierced his thought, released his ideas and, once again, words flowed. Leaving the drawing to itself, he wrote.

'Molten caverns glow.
Black mountains forbid.
Light flickers,
spits, spurts,
crackling blue, sizzling orange,
and is gone.

Soft yellows, pale, wavering,
bend to evaporate
into vast darkness.

Warm embers glow on,
slowly wane.
Deepening caverns merge,
cinders split, cool,
petrify.'

Satisfied that he was at last unchained, Sentinel wandered outside, into the cool of evening beginning and walked the paved road to the shore. He stood as soft damp caressed his features. Refreshed, he waited while day faded to obscurity and night emerged. His thoughts belonged to Sentinel; his own thoughts and his own ideas; precious, safe.
"They cannot be snatched."

Some days passed in calm reflection. It was early. Sentinel set out. The day had dawned, soft with gently caressing air and the promise of blue skies. His path took him to the shore, a stony, pebbled shore where his feet moved quietly across larger stones but disturbed the pebbles further on to bursts of percussion; these joined the suck and lap of the sea and the still air. It seemed a transitory beating of time, waiting for a new phrase to begin. He smiled at the thought and lifted his head to gaze along the shoreline.

In the distance, but not too far away, he watched a girl; no, a woman; standing at the edge of the sea looking out towards the horizon. To Sentinel, she belonged to the scene as a figure in a painting. He sat on the shingle and ran pebbles between his fingers, watched this movement for a while before he turned his head to look back to where the woman had stood. Now, she was treading carefully his way, raising her skirt a little and concentrating on her steps. The sea licked her ankles.

Sentinel concentrated, too, focussing on the stream of pebbles he was lifting and sifting. He kept his head down. To view as if studying a painting was a pleasure; to encounter the reality, a small torture.

He heard the woman pass, smelled vague fragrance, did not look up. Neither did she acknowledge Sentinel. So, why a wistful sigh in his heart when it should pound with relief?

"If it had been a different day, not a solitary one, I would have looked up, smiled a greeting, or lifted a hand in the gesture of a wave," he thought and did not consider that she may not have wanted to acknowledge him.

When she was at a safe distance from him, Sentinel stood, stretched and wandered back along the way he had come.

"This day can continue on a calm note," being the thought that spurred him to begin living it.

Chapter Five

Maggie

Maggie is the name of the woman on the shore, an inner rebel ill composed to being at large in this world of regulations and chants. Her mind constructed a wall to shut out those annoyances; a wall behind which she chose to live.

Solitary, even as a child, Maggie preferred to be remote from what she claimed to be the machine of the world, rather than a part of it; an observer. She embarked on the construction of the wall, stone by stone, early on when all around her became a mismatch; not fitting; an unsolvable puzzle. The stones wedged; like dry stone walling, they were virtually indestructible.

She viewed her childhood as an apprenticeship for adult life.

"Hone it now and it will bear you through whatever the future holds," she told herself many a time.

Satisfied that her fortress would become impregnable, she felt able to rebel in small ways at first and often rebellion of the mind; this would be the base for years ahead.

Every now and then, Maggie attempted to rationalise the incomprehensibility of adults. For too long and too often had she witnessed and heard destructive behaviour, bludgeoning words.

An only child who had not attended nursery school, she spent much time, early on, in the company of adults; time she engineered to be as little as possible as she shut them out from her small, precious world; a world she had no desire to share and would not allow them to destroy as they chose to destroy themselves and others.

The city outskirts did not afford much in the way of natural life, mainly hard slabs of pavement and the smell of melting tar in hot weather. But, on looking up, chimney pots cut into the skyline, shone a brilliant orange-red against the blue on sunny days. Pollarded trees, tight fisted during winter, sprouted small, soft canopies of leaves in spring. The trees were sparsely set into the paving but, in full leaf, broke the tedium of lifeless colour.

Maggie's feet burned as she slap-slapped in sandals, pounding the road to school, desiring to become as fast as the wind; almost a reality in the 'in between' – the road there and the road back – that mattered so much to her. Within that space of time, Maggie found freedom to breathe; a space between two sets of rules.

"Present," each chanted as the register was called. Did one have to be present? Could one answer but be absent all the same, in a rogue country or floating with the clouds?

And then the routine set in.

Maggie recalled the day she had collected pebbles on the journey. There was a large pile at the side of the road, beside a driveway. She chose those that appealed, in colour and according to smoothness and shape (although there was not much difference in shape, nor size). She stayed too long in her choosing, was late, her pockets heavy, jingling. The teacher noticed.

"Have you been stealing?"

"No," answered Maggie.

"Empty your pockets,"

"No," retorted Maggie.

"Do as I say!"

"Won't!"

A sharp smack.

"Empty them!"

Maggie had stood, furious, trapped. Delving suddenly, with both hands, into her two pockets, she filled each hand fat, withdrew them and threw the pebbles as far as she could across the floor.

A moment of horrifying silence.

"There! If you want them, pick them up!"

She had stood before the headmistress accused of insolence and thieving.

"I found them," she said.

"You took them, stole them," she was told.

No one really trusted her after that. To be branded a thief at six carried a sentence of whispers and sly glances.

'Never trust a thief.'

She screwed up the words and tossed them out.

"I am not a thief," she told herself. "I am Maggie."

From that day, she began to find herself.

Choice

'Of all the souls that stand create
I have elected one ...'

Emily Dickinson

Chapter Six

Spindel

Released from the chasm, I return to those palaces of glass, that city of glass palaces, not knowing another way to go, and see that I met a prince there. I resurrect them and move forwards, a wraith lured towards a destiny; my own or that of another. I cannot tell. And did I meet that prince, or is he ahead of me? Am I repeating a phrase, or is this a new motif? These are questions and the answers are obscured.

Cold air meets my approach. I am as breath on a window pane.
Is that my entire substance; that breath left behind, exhaled by a more solid form? I pause, but do not reflect at this moment in time; the search for the symphony is my driving force. I do not consider time; although it lurks in the shadows at the edge of my mind; not today.

I move stealthily; as breath. I do not wish to disturb my thoughts; they must remain intact. I recall my reflection, in an earlier time, in those palaces of glass; the act of being mirrored. But there was more. I did not perceive this at that time. My senses combine to recall it, now.

A shape, a shade perhaps, lingering on the air. A haunting

presence which I shut out. Was it the cold freezing it out, or did my mind decline to receive it, then?

The questions take their own route, form a questioning phrase of bars which ponder the notes before moving swiftly on. This music is tricky, as water over pebbles, stalling, uneven, rapid; an exciting phrase to awaken the attention.

I am close, almost reaching the point at which I rested previously, but remain on the outskirts of the city; a voyeur.

Parsu, a prince, sees a form, a beautiful silhouette against the skyline of a setting sun. The sun goes down suddenly in this country; darkness descends and the form is lost.

He sees it in his dreams that night; conjures it to pass before him once more. He lends it music so as to watch it dance, this time alight with the colours of a flame, against a background of pitch. Wondrously, the shape bends and flows, flickers and darts, caressing the darkness as a lover.

Parsu awakens with a start. He desires that elusive figure, that flame, that silhouette. Find it he must; it has become his heart's desire. The task will not be an easy one. To search diligently, secretly; he does not want the silhouetted form to evade him a second time. He will ask questions, listen carefully, wait patiently. For all his power, for all his wealth and influence, he cannot demand her presence. Humbled; no longer a prince but a seeker, he knows this … one day she will become his princess.

The dream sequence ends. I, Spindel, allow a sigh to pass. It is time to move from night skies and palaces of glass, for now. A different yearning draws my mind from a vision which could become a fixation. I withdraw as a veil, once again, mists the scene. I slide out; back to light and warmth. Winter has passed this time around. Spring has arrived.

I am on a path; a path that takes me beside a soft grass bank, bright in the light of day. I rest there, calm, pensive. A bud unfolds; begins its day of blossoming. The vestiges of that earlier vision linger at the edge of memory. I drift into sleep.

Time moves on.

I wake to the glory of that flower, fully unfurled. Sit enthralled; see parts, many parts equalling a whole; petals in a circle creating the corolla, pistil, stamens and the calyx drawing them together to form a delicate vibrancy. My symphony is to be such; the drawing together of parts to create that which is complete; perfect. It can evolve.

I ponder on the thought of a part combining with parts to become another; a separate identity yet containing those parts.

I sense a figure approaching along the distance of the path, disturbing my thought. I watch. I wait. Is this figure a dream, a figment? Perhaps. It takes a feminine form; beauty in enigmatic mode; magnetic in soft movement and inner glow which reaches me as I sit; wait for her to close the space between us.

Standing, I step into her path.

"My name is Spindel."

"Mine Segment."

She smiles. I watch her and step aside. I do not wish to bar her way.

"This path will serve you well," she tells me as she pauses for longer than I had anticipated, "but you are headed in the wrong direction."

"I know my way," I reply, "and you appear to know yours."

"I am returning. You are moving towards confusion, doubt. It brings misery."

"For you, maybe," I acknowledge, "but not necessarily for me." Segment smiles at me.

"Make your choice, Spindel."

She turns to move away, pursue her path.

"Wait! Will you take this path again? Will we meet at another time, in another place?"

"Do you want me to accompany you?" she asks.

I consider.

"You could?" An enquiry.

"If that is your need."

Suddenly, it is my desperate need.

"It is."

"Then I shall come with you; not for ease, neither yours nor mine, but because you have chosen this destiny."

"Where were you headed?" I ask.

"Towards my own," she answers. "As I said, my name is Segment. I am one of many. I was returning to my own."

I think that I hear a note of torture within her words. I dismiss it. It is not for now.

"Come with me."

Segment turns. I leave the grassy bank. She follows. I have her in mind.

The flower, so delicate, wilts in the strength of the sun.

※

Segment sleeps, curved into the indentation of a smooth root, as if a part of it. As she sleeps, I, Spindel, query. 'One of many' – what does that signify? In my mind I dwell on this. Is each of us one of many? Yes. But I feel that Segment's words contain a diversity; a different significance that I cannot hold in my mind. There are many beings and, in this, we are inextricably linked, but loosely in that we are bound on one planet. Minds. There are many minds to fit the many beings; are these inextricably linked? I, Spindel, think not.

For what do I search; an answer or a meaning?

Segment stirs, sighs, flutters her eyes to wake. Is she a part of me?

We journey on. At times she darts ahead; a trill of demi-semi quavers; at others lingers by the edge of the path, gazing; a sustained minim; a breve. I collect these notes and give them quality, deep, haunting, tense with delight.

Chapter Seven

Sentinel

Sentinel bound himself to the calm that he had found, as if it was a pillow of down that he carried; lay with it, absorbed the softness of its form. This was how he visualised the calm; cloud-like in quality.

He began his day in earnest, sorting notes, placing odd drawings in a folder, but not labelling it; this would confine the drawings within. Each breath a breath of hope, each thought and movement coherent. He decided to paint a wall of his room; to create a mural.

Using music as a backdrop and colour as notes, Sentinel stroked the wall with brushes, formed waves rolling softly, in tranquil rhythm, towards a pebbled shore. In strong, round movements his brush formed glistening pebbles for the sea to reach for and the sky lay waiting for the sun to paint its colours.

Hours passed into two days, with breaks for food and sleep. Satisfied, Sentinel studied his creation, rested in his calm.

※

Under the influence of this calm and the portrayal of such before his eyes, Sentinel completed assignments, reached goals and succeeded in his every effort. Buoyed by consistency, he floated between height and depth; felt them ever present, hovering but not touching.

On an even day, he took himself confidently to the shore to scrunch his way towards the stone pier in the distance. Breathing deeply and feeling the breeze press against him, he strode on. There were others walking, sitting, standing; in contemplation of the horizon, perhaps. He passed them by. And then he saw her, that same woman, skirt hitched slightly, feet hidden in the foam. Her hair blew outwards, wisped, dancing in the breeze; as an instrument played haphazardly, attempting to discover rhythm.

Sentinel laughed; to himself, he thought, but it must have been voiced and he was much nearer to her than he had supposed; alarmingly near. She turned.

"It *is* a happy day, isn't it?" she smiled back at him.

"Yes," he answered, dropping his head slightly.

"Did I interrupt your thoughts?"

"Yes. No. I mean, no," spoke Sentinel and surprised himself in adding, "I am enjoying walking, the sound of the pebbles, the splash of the waves – even the gulls calling."
He waved his hand vaguely towards where two or three wheeled with precision high above them.

"I like the feel of the sea between my toes, around my feet."
She stepped out of the water, closer.

"Must be fun," said Sentinel.

"It is. Try it; sometime," she added, sensing his reluctance to feel entirely free, to be coerced.

"Maybe,"

She slid her feet into slight sandals that she had left lying at the edge of the sea's domain. Sentinel took a step, as if to move on.

"Shall I walk with you?" she enquired. "I am headed in the same direction, to the pier. Say if you mind, only you look as if company would be good for you."

Sentinel suddenly felt freed of his inhibition.

"Yes, join me," he answered.

"You needn't talk, not if you don't want to. We can just walk alongside."

Sentinel smiled his appreciation at her thoughtfulness and then,

"We can talk – and walk," he told her.

"Well, I'm Maggie. Who are you?"

Sentinel hesitated. He was about to give his name, his public name, when he realised that he would be Sentinel to her; to Maggie.

"Sentinel," he offered.

"That's unusual," commented Maggie.

"Yes."

They began their walk to the pier smiling, glancing at one another,

"I saw you once before." Sentinel spoke first. "Here."

"And I saw you, Sentinel – I love the sound of your name. I need to keep saying it." Maggie laughed. "You were sitting, pretending not to look, but I knew you were."

"Sorry."

"Don't be. I felt drawn to you, then, but I sensed that you wouldn't have wanted me to call out, acknowledge you."

"True," he answered, "then."

"And now?"

"Now is different. Now is a good time. Do you live here?"

"No. Not really. At the moment, but not always."

"Oh."

Maggie and Sentinel continued, for a while, in silence.

"The pier. We're almost there," Maggie pointed out. "Race you!"

She set off as fast as the pebbles would allow. Sentinel gasped, horrified by her spontaneity … and then relaxed, following at a lumbering pace; a shire horse following a fallow deer.

When Sentinel arrived, Maggie had already scrambled up the rocks onto the jetty; it was that more than a pier. She sat clasping her knees, the wind catching her hair in that wild chaotic dance. He climbed to stand beside her.

"Sit!" she commanded.

Obedient, he sat.

"You made it," laughed Maggie.

"I did," laughed Sentinel.

"And was it fun?"

"It was sudden, but yes, fun," agreed Sentinel.

"Are you from here, or are you, too, passing through?"

"I'm studying and working, so I live here at the moment. I don't know where I shall be in a year or two."

"Does anyone? This is a fragment of our time. Let's enjoy it,"

Maggie announced.

Caught unawares, Sentinel showed his alarm. Maggie smiled, leaned and touched his arm.

"I'm not trying to trap you. Think of it this way. We are passing clouds sharing the same piece of sky. We will change shape. The wind will carry us in different directions – we may disappear entirely – but, for now, we are sharing both time and space – an hour, several hours. What do you think?"

Sentinel squinted at Maggie in the sunlight, both perplexed and intrigued.

"Well." Maggie jumped up. "Let's go to the end of the pier, gaze out to sea, see how we feel."

She set off. Sentinel, standing now, followed, caught up, took her hand.

"Thank you," he said.

Maggie looked directly into his eyes; her own smiling.

At the end of the pier they stood, quite still, watching the movement of the water, the scudding clouds; felt the strengthening wind push against them.

"Maggie."

Sentinel caught her arms, turned her and buried his head in the essence of her being; breathed the aroma of her clothes, skin. And gently sobbed.

For some time they remained silhouetted against the skyline, lost in each other, the dance of the wind, the lament of the gulls and the soft beat of time passing.

✵

When he thought back to that day, he remembered Maggie's words.

"Relief," she said, "pure relief."

And it had been; the sheer beauty of the whole experience written in his memory, transposed.

Chapter Eight

Maggie

One day, when she was almost fourteen, her father had gone.
"Gone where?"
Not a question to be asked.
"Gone."
Maggie took it at its value – a word with no sentiment, not much significance; a flat, ugly word.
"So what?" she retorted.
"Don't care then."
"I won't."
Maggie turned and left the kitchen.

※

Now, he is dead; cremated; is nowhere. This she discovered in a few words spoken when she passed by her mother's house (for that is what it is) that he had left a cottage; 'more a shack' were the words.
"So that's where he went."
"It must be sold."
Maggie determined to visit prior to this event; made preparation, telling no one.

※

Finding the cottage proved relatively easy and Maggie drove to the area as soon as she could. She had no key; posed as a prospective buyer, under a false name; viewed it.

The agent left the keys on a table. Maggie distracted him, asking for more information than was provided. He stepped outside to phone the office. Maggie worked a key from the ring. There was more than one for both front and back doors; the keyring old. She hoped that he would not notice; until later. He did not. Maggie thanked him for his efforts, shook his hand; said that she would be in touch.

With a duplicate key, she returned and dropped the original key to the floor before she locked up and drove off. There would be time to return at leisure, to claim his space for a while.

※

The cottage; not by any description a shack; stands at the end of an unmade lane of stones, compacted earth and grass vying for superiority. Two semi detached cottages mark the turn-off to the lane; obviously holiday rentals. A short street of terraced houses, with a gap of land taken up by small allotments, leads past the lane to join the road into the seaside town. Possibly, they were built originally for labourers, along with the cottages. Except for one, they are not well kept.

At the end of the lane, encroaching slightly on the cottage, is a coppice of trees that could well have been planted for protection from sea winds crossing the open fields beyond; fields fallow or carrying this year's crop of kale or wheat.

Maggie assessed the area as she walked from her car, parked on the main street, carrying a backpack holding necessary clothes and provisions. She felt the key in her pocket; grasped it more firmly as she approached. There had been no visible neighbours around and she had not witnessed curtains twitching as she passed.

※

A day earlier, she had exchanged the time of day with an elderly lady snipping dead foliage in her garden. Maggie had asked about the cottage; who owned it?

The lady, Mrs Flynn, widowed, told her of the gentleman who *had* lived there. A few months before his death, her neighbours thought that he was moving out. He had hired a skip. She did not, herself, go that way, did not get about much; bad legs but good enough to hold her up for a bit of gardening and her neighbours looked out for her. The man kept himself to himself. He had died in hospital, so had not been alone. Had he died in his bed, no one would have known; would have thought him living elsewhere. She added these points with great effect.

"That's good – that he was not alone," agreed Maggie. "Is it for sale then?"

"Seems as if it is,"

"Thank you. I'll walk down and have a look."

"Lovely day!"

"It is. Thank you." Maggie waved a goodbye as she walked off.

With the pretence of heading towards the lane, intent on entering it, she had hurried back out and set off, right, into the town, to the agent; to feign disinterest in the property.

She decided to approach from this other direction in future as a slight curve in the road, she had noticed, precluded Mrs Flynn from seeing who entered the lane. The holiday cottages appeared conveniently vacant.

※

As she closed in on the cottage, Maggie glanced behind to make sure that she was unobserved; grasped the key in her pocket, tightly. Another glance down the lane as she slotted the key into the lock; clicked open the door.

She stood in the hallway and realised that she had taken in few details before; her focal intention had been to obtain a key. The stairs lay ahead and, to the right, four coat hooks mounted on a piece of wood screwed to the wall. What air there was smelled stale. Maggie pushed open the door to the sitting room, which had only been pulled to.

The sitting room held few objects. Her Dad (for that was what he was to her; not father; too grand a word) had almost cleared the place. In readiness for death? She could only speculate.

A lone armchair sat beside a small table with a lamp standing on it. At the far end, but not far away, she observed a bare dining table and two ill matched chairs. Against the wall, to the left, an empty bookcase.

"Who were you?" she pondered.

In the kitchen, off to the right, Maggie found only basic pans, crockery and utensils; enough to cater for life; short term.

There were two bedrooms above and what appeared to be a toilet and bathroom both in their original state; ideal for a 'kitchen sink' drama, she smiled to herself. One of the bedrooms, that at the front, stood bare, while the other housed a single bed and a utility wardrobe containing a few clothes. In the airing cupboard some well worn sheets, towels and pillow cases lay redundant.

Retreating downstairs, Maggie looked out at the back, through the window in the kitchen door. She saw a shed, standing as if waiting for action, on the gravel and grass patch that hardly lived up to the name 'lawn'.

Unable to access the back, Maggie stole back out at the front, key in hand and pushed through overgrown redcurrant and privet. The shed door was closed but not locked. Grateful, she grasped the handle and prised open the rusted hinges that guarded against intrusion. The contents became immediately visible. The shed held tools, mainly rusted, and an old pair of stepladders.

"So that's what you were guarding," she told it and grinned. "Your treasure."

Maggie pushed the door back into place.

"You can keep it," she said and returned to the cottage.

"And that is it," she spoke into the silence inside and breathed out a sigh.

"You became nothing; no one. Was that your desire?" she asked an absent Dad.

"I'll stay for a while, Dad, if you don't mind; get some feel of you before you are totally obliterated."

"The electron in an atom cannot rotate round the atomic nucleus as the Earth rotates round the sun, or else it would soon radiate its energy and fall into the nucleus'

Shan Gao

Chapter Nine

Spindel

I, Spindel, follow Segment. She passes quickly along the path. I look neither left nor right; rapt in the confidence of her movement.

Suddenly, she stops, turns; faces me. We almost collide; a soft clash of cymbals. Stop. Her eyes meet mine. I am drawn in; through the iris to the pupil.

※

I am in a grove, a grove of almond trees laden with blossom. The heady scent of honeyed pollen cascades; a million bees drone in unison; a lullaby; a potion. My senses overwhelmed, I float free; intoxicated.

The path is somewhere that I am not.

※

I travel, yet do not move. I cling; to what? All is intangible. Do I cling to sound? Is this a possibility? Can I hang on a note as a clapper hangs from a bell?

※

Pain; eventually I experience the pain of intensity. I must let go; do not. Desire pressures me on; upwards into a grey mass that envelopes all. No sound, no scent, no note to which to cling. I am without an anchor; an echo reverberating to eternity; or extinction.

※

I, Spindel, leave; do not leave. Some thing draws my presence downwards. I do not plummet but tumble, heavily; no semblance of direction. My plea, in the numbness of my mind, to hesitate; grasp a moment on which to hold a thought.

※

A sob. I hear a sob; sobbing; an entire soul sobbing for itself.
I realise. I, Spindel, am that soul. I sob for myself; and cannot stop.

Chapter Ten

Maggie

Maggie mounted the stairs to take clothes from her backpack; dump them on the bed.

"That's it," she told herself; stepped over the threshold into the back bedroom.

"Or is it?" she realised and backed out.

On the small landing, she looked up again; a trapdoor; to the water tank, she supposed.

"The ladders."

Maggie threw her backpack into the bedroom and headed downstairs. How to get them inside was the question. The importance, not to be seen.

"Does that dining room window open?" she wondered aloud; ran to try it.

"Yes. Maybe I can get them through it."

She pulled a chair over to the window, dropped onto the concrete strip outside and returned to the shed.

"Sorry," she told it, "I don't always mean what I say."

Maggie carried the ladders and pushed them through into the dining room. She pulled herself up and in after them.

Negotiating the narrow doorway and hall, an exercise in

itself, she pushed the ladders upwards, keeping her weight behind them to prevent backsliding.

The loft cover lifted and could be easily pushed to the side. Maggie levered herself up into the loft space and stood beside the water tank.

"You *are* here," she addressed it.

It was too dark to see far, but the loft appeared to be empty. She lowered herself down to fetch a torch from the backpack; climbed back up.

Nothing. Something; a tan suitcase from bygone years. Maggie crawled forward, fearful of putting a hole in the ceiling; stretched an arm to reach out; dragged it towards her. It was heavy, but not heavy enough to weigh her down, nor to cause damage to the ceiling. How to get it down? She cast her mind back to the shed; recalled a piece of rope hanging on a hook to the side.

Maggie lowered herself down to the landing and ran downstairs to exit through the dining room window once more; this time to collect the rope that she hoped she had not conveniently imagined.

Back at the top of the stepladders, she fastened the rope to the handle of the suitcase, climbed into the loft and lowered the case gently to the landing. Back on the steps, she pulled the trapdoor cover into place and climbed down.

The suitcase, minus the rope that had been tied to the handle, was left, temporarily, on the landing and she struggled with the stepladders and rope, returning them to the shed.

"I am not a thief," she told the shed; and the memory flooded in that, to some, that *was* what she was thought to be. Maggie shrugged, wedged shut the shed door, climbed in through the dining room window and closed it.

"Now."

She carried the suitcase down the stairs; placed it on the dining table. The catches were rusted; she tried them; locked, perhaps? With a few wrenches from a screwdriver lying in the kitchen drawer they were easy to prise open.

※

More time had passed than Maggie had realised. She felt pangs of hunger, also a reluctance to open the case.

She must be organised. The suitcase lying on the table, the backpack in the bedroom; what if the agent returned? Prior to this moment, she had not worked out the practicalities of staying in the cottage. She would need to make up the bed and draw the cover over the evidence of her existence each day. Where to store food? There was no fridge; the agent or clients guaranteed to open drawers and cupboards. She had not considered whether or not the water had been left on, nor how she would erase traces of her using it. A torch countered the need for electricity. She could not allow light to shine out; nor could she cook here; boil that rickety kettle, perhaps, in the evening to allow it to cool by morning.

"I should have put more thought into this; not arrived on a whim driven by determination to salvage something of a person who was/is Dad," she told herself as she poked around in the backpack to find a banana and a few biscuits that she knew were in there.

Maggie found them, stuffed the backpack into hiding, behind an old stained pillow, on the shelf of the wardrobe, and ran downstairs.

"Rubbish," she thought as she peeled the banana. "Where to put it?"

Rooting in the kitchen drawer, she came across a neatly folded paper bag, poking out from beneath the plastic cutlery container.

"This will do." She pushed the banana skin into the bag and carried it with her to the sitting room.

Maggie peeped through the window at the front, moving the net slightly. There was no sign of imminent visitors. The agent would soon shut up shop for the day.

She returned to the table. She must summon the courage to look inside the case before it became too dark. Maggie sat on one of the chairs and tentatively lifted the lid of the suitcase. Photographs. She could see the edge of an exercise book; like those she had used in primary school. There were a few scraps of paper with scribbles that looked like lists; shopping lists, notes for the milkman? Had there been one? She would discover their contents soon; first the photographs.

The photographs were of herself, as a baby; later a child. She stood with her Dad, mostly. Her mother must have been the photographer. A few were taken with her mother, but her mother looked away, outside the scene. In some, Maggie stood alone; occasion photographs; a birthday, new school uniform, a Christmas dress.

"My legacy," she thought; felt sad but detached.

She found some other photographs of her Dad smiling, happy, with her mother when she was young. And yet, it was not quite her mother; the lips not the same, nor the eyes of this mother; bright and filled with young love. She turned them over. The name, in fountain pen on the back, not her mother's.

Maggie stopped searching, laid out photographs of herself and her mother alongside those of this other woman; gathered them up again. She took the suitcase of photographs to the bedroom; the notebook and scraps of paper in her hand. Her intention was to read these by torchlight; in bed.

Thankful that the bed was in the back room, she quickly made it up. At the window hung a heavy curtain which could be drawn; privacy that afforded solace in the maze of puzzles and confusion that her former life dangled before her; jeering.

Chapter Eleven

Sentinel

That memorable day, Maggie had touched him tenderly; in reassurance. She had looked into his eyes, which were blurred with tears; had kissed his nose and had run away, lightly; a leaf blown by the wind.

Sentinel allowed shame to descend; as a fog of mist rolling in on the sea. He stood, unwilling to move. Eventually, he had turned, looked along the shore; Maggie had gone.

He had remained in his room for days, eating only when necessary, and felt that he was melting, slowly, into oblivion.

"How could I have done that?" he chastised himself; over and over.

He *had* sobbed; it could never be erased.

※

Now, that bereft experience had faded; Maggie, only the sensation of Maggie, remained. Each day, he hoped; hoped that he would find her. And, if he did not? Still, the precious memory remained.

※

He queued to buy bread at a local bakery; the smell of the interior enticing his appetite. His mind was nowhere; not possessed by a particular thought. Just pending.

"Sentinel."

The sound of his name, spoken softly. He turned. Maggie touched his arm, gently; smiled.

"I didn't mean to alarm you."

He smiled until it became a grin.

"Maggie!" he responded

"Who else," she replied.

Sentinel laughed.

"No one."

'No one' also his thought as no other person knew his name; not that name.

"Let's buy bread – cake, too – have a picnic on the pebbles."

Sentinel looked at Maggie; attempted to take in her suggestion.

"You can do that, Sentinel," she told him. "And I still love to say your name."

They chose cake, bought bread and left the bakery hand in hand; school children on an outing.

"Fun?" Maggie asked.

"Fun," responded Sentinel and allowed a grin to spread. "Yes. Fun," he affirmed and in the saying of it, told himself this truth.

"We need ham – or something," said Maggie as she stopped outside a delicatessen.

"Hmm." Sentinel fell in with her mood. "Always ham on a picnic."

They laughed.

"Wine, too," she encouraged.

"Wine," echoed Sentinel.

It felt easy to walk together, as if he had walked for years with Maggie; since time began. But new to him; a discovery.

"Maggie."

She tilted her head towards him.

"Maggie. Can I ask why you are here?"

"No," she answered, shaking her head. "Not today, Sentinel. Today is for us; no past intrusions."

"I understand."

"Today is who we are today, Sentinel; not who we were, nor who we will be. Strange?"

"No, Maggie, not strange. I understand. Believe me, I understand."

"Then that is how it is – today."

"An unexplored 'today'"

"It's music that we make – music that has not been played before, Sentinel."

"Why music, Maggie?"

"Music has no beginning, no end. It can come from nowhere, plays on, accumulates, becomes ….."

"Becomes what?"

Maggie faltered.

"I don't know. I don't know why I said that." She looked distressed, but for only a moment. "Just today, Sentinel. Just today."

"Yes." Sentinel thought that he understood.

"Thank you." Maggie squeezed his hand. He grasped hers in reassurance, as she had reassured him on that first 'today'.
They walked on.

Waves crashed and sucked greedily at the pebbles. The sun hid. Clouds raced; playthings of the wind. Maggie zipped her jacket.

"Over here," Sentinel beckoned.
Above the pebbles, grasses and gorse peppered the uneven lie of the land.

"There's a dip, Maggie – a sheltered place. I have hidden here before."

"Hidden? From what?"
For an instant, Sentinel found himself a child; himself in his childhood shelter.

"No. Not hidden." He laughed it off. "Sheltered – a place to sit and wait for the world to pass."

"And did it?"

"Not exactly, but I escaped for a while."

"You're happy to share it?"

"With you. Yes. I think so. No. I *know* so."

They reached the dip and scuttled into the shelter of its curved bank. The picnic lay in bags beside them.

"Our haven!" pronounced Maggie.
A frown crossed her brow.

"Sentinel. Your name is so beautiful. Is it your real name? Have I asked you that before?"

"Yes. It is my real name."

Sentinel did not lie. The name that others claimed to be his, a false name.

"Sentinel," Maggie repeated his name. "A haven is never for always. I think you know that, Sentinel – that it is for a space of time only."

"Well, today, Maggie – and you did say that today is for us – this is our haven – our refuge from the world. We are ourselves, here."

"Are we?"

In that instant, Sentinel became aware that Maggie knew differently; an electric panic danced within him.

'To any action there is always an opposite and equal reaction'

Sir Isaac Newton

Chapter Twelve

Spindel

Tears that have become crystals; crystalline. They lie, sprinkled, on the ground. A day is dawning; a dark day, but the sun glints between two massive banks of cloud; a sun with strength that melts those crystal-like forms to leave rims of salt on the path.

I, Spindel, am pressurised by cloud weight. Fearful of being trapped between the two banks of cloud; as grapes in a wine press; I edge towards the shelter of a rock that juts out, provides a place to hide until the pressure eases. I am in a place where Segment is not; in another time; perhaps.

※

Again, I dream, as I crouch in hiding; spiral dizzily attempting to catch meaning; purpose. Confusion reigns; a curtain of rain pours before me from the slope of the rock. The dream spreads, draws me in its surge, and I wade out, into its sphere.

The plain is dry and flat, but there is a town, or some such place, in the distance. I tread; continue to tread. The road lies as an abandoned ribbon on the plain. The road takes me quickly; the distance decreases and I enter the town; for that is what it is.

I breathe in spices that lace the air with bitter-sweet fragrance, and I see an open garden ahead, laid out formally in curves, not angles. It creates a soft balance against the austerity of the surrounding stone buildings. Prince Parsu is seated there, in that garden. I see him clearly.

I, Spindel, am in that same garden. I stand; watch from beneath the shade of overhanging branches laden with leaves.

He is waiting. Towards him walks his dream's desire; that silhouetted figure who has captured his heart; whose heart he desires.

I hear her voice. It rings delicately upon the air; a tinkle of small bells.

"Prince Parsu. I am here at your request. Why?"

Her voice sets simple words, carefully chosen. She omits herself; apart from the 'I'. Her name hangs, invisible, waiting.

"Sit beside me," answers the prince.

He indicates a vacant space on the stone bench. She crosses; sits; looks ahead at a small fountain; not at Prince Parsu.

"Tell me your name," he invites.

She turns her head to the side; deliberately; to catch his gaze.

"I believe you know my name. How else could you find me and summon me?"

"I do not," he replies, but does not answer her question.

Two unanswered questions lie between them.

"My name is Olmi," she concedes.

"Olmi." Prince Parsu speaks her name softly, allowing it to

linger on the air; no longer invisible. It is a sound; a breath.

"Olmi," he repeats. "Beautiful," he adds.

"Why am I here?" asks Olmi.

"I cannot say," he admits.

They sit in silence; in the garden. The garden continues to make its own music of birds and fountains, breezes and leaves; insects a constant background rhythm.

"Olmi," Prince Parsu repeats in a whisper, after some several minutes.

"Olmi," spoken in strength; desire. He leans towards her, takes her hands in his.

"Olmi. You are my desire."

"How?" Puzzled, Olmi continues, "You don't know me. We have not met – until now."

"You are in my dreams, Olmi. That is not enough, was never enough. Now, you are here. My dreams have awakened."

Olmi withdraws her hands. Stands.

"I am no one's dream. I am myself, Prince Parsu."

"Stay," he pleads. "Stay. I cannot live alone, without you."

He bends forward, covering his face with his hands; visibly disturbed

Olmi sits; gently removes his hands from his face.

"I do not mean to hurt you, but we are strangers, Prince Parsu."

Prince Parsu gazes steadily into her eyes.

"Since the night I saw your form, silhouetted, you have been mine. Here in my heart." His right hand clutches at his breast.

A servant appears bringing sweet meats; another bearing tea. Olmi sits, her back erect; poised; waiting to receive her destiny.

I, Spindel, withdraw as a wraith; leave the scene of my fascination; drift.

※

I wake. My heart strings taut; each breath, tense. I experience tearing within my breast; moan, scratch at the earth for solace.

Unbearable pain; a journey of unbearable pain. Is it my own?

Chapter Thirteen

Sentinel

Sentinel sat in his room, the soft glow of remembrance caressing him; firelight dancing in the hearth of his childhood. This flame, too, all consuming; his desire, to be consumed.

Today had passed; yesterday. There is always tomorrow. Maggie had said that she would find him 'perhaps before I have found myself', she had joked; so it seemed. Sentinel had caught a hard edge at the back of her voice; mocking not himself, Sentinel, but Maggie, in self mockery. A voice that he did not want to be a part of the memory of 'Maggie of today'; but was.

Concerned, he had reached out in an attempt to grasp just one grain of her inner being; the moment lost as she turned to methodically tidy the scraps of their picnic. Lost, he now realised, because he did not know how to claim it; had not the strength to be what he hoped to become. Not on that picnic; that today.

They had walked back into the town. He had indicated where he was living, for now. Maggie had smiled.

"Thank you," she said, touching his wrist.

She had known that in so doing he had parted with a small portion of his anonymity; had given it to her.

As they parted, he had not asked where she was going; had not looked back to see which direction, left or right, she had taken at the corner; respected her need for privacy.

But, they had shared; in that hollow; their bodies, their souls in a silent pledge, with passion and depth of feeling such as he had never known; drawn together to become one; today.

Together, they had become another; strong, assured; that could continue forever. The initial phrase of a prelude; minims and quavers of delight obscuring underlying pain.

Sentinel paused at this direction of his thought. He could visualise those notes of delight. Could they be drawn? A sensuous backdrop. What colours appeared, merged, parted before his eyes; notes dancing, almost pirouetting to impart the tune. And would an observer of that work experience the music? His question hovered before him. Idly, his pencil moved across the page.

Chapter Fourteen

Maggie

Maggie had returned that day, by car, to the cottage. Today.

"Why?" She chastised herself. "What did I do? Why?" In a Greek drama she would rent her clothes, tear at her hair; she felt.

"I am cruel. I am not a thief, but I am cruel," she told herself. "Or am I a thief? Have I stolen something, something precious from him; from Sentinel. No. He gave it freely, but I gave nothing in return."

Somewhere, deep within, a discord twanged; challenging that supposition. In denial, she held onto the cruelty she supposed; a pattern, a motif, constantly repeated since early childhood.

Bringing down the suitcase, Maggie forced herself to open it. The knowledge of Sentinel washed over her. She beat the table with her fist, sank onto the nearest old chair. Her head fell forward. She cradled it in her arms and cried into the table top; the suitcase an ominous presence.

Minutes later, she pushed the chair from the table and ran to the kitchen tap. She splashed her eyes and face with cold water; rubbed them dry. Maggie stamped a foot in temper.

"Don't do it!" she scolded aloud. "Don't! Just don't do it – ever again!"

She made her vow in silence; to be alone, beholden to none. "Not even Sentinel," came the after thought, which vaporised as swiftly as it had occurred.

"The suitcase." Maggie determined to focus on the suitcase; to discover the woman, not her mother, who stood with her father in his youthful days; before her birth.

These photographs lay on the top, where she had placed them. She studied Margaret (that was her name, the same as her own; almost) carefully. Noted her facial features. Looked at those of her mother; similar, but not exactly the same. Sisters. Perhaps they were sisters; although she had no Aunt Margaret. There was never an aunt around; nor an uncle.

Margaret appeared gay; an old fashioned word but appropriate for that time and carefree in her manner; as opposed to her mother; determined, obstinate. Mabel, her mother's name; its sound to Maggie, as a child, that of a bluebell softly ringing. A hope for her mother that was not to be; as yet.

"Is there always hope?" Maggie doubted it in this instance.

She could take the photographs; ask her mother. But she knew that it would never happen. Placing the photographs to one side, Maggie began to lift each item in turn; examine the interest it afforded. Mostly, there were more photographs. She did not want further visual clutter in her mind. Underneath these lay scraps of paper with odd notes scribbled in pencil. Some, lists of household goods, food items, presumably to shop for.

"So this is how he lived, ate," she mused, assuming that they were in his handwriting. Some contained short phrases; mystifying; as if a part of a poem, or letter. But why on scraps of paper?

'I miss you M'
'always – you are always there'
'I cannot bear to think"
'I wish – so often I wish'
'she reminds me – too much she reminds me'
'M M M '
'a tear in my heart'

"Is that a tear cried or a heart rent?"
It was too sad; after 'today'; too sad to continue.

"My Dad was not who I supposed. Who was M? Margaret? Mabel? Certainly not Maggie."

The day would soon draw to a close. Maggie returned both scraps and photographs to the suitcase. And hid it at the back of the cupboard under the stairs. She crawled into the black, musty space and backed out. Latched the door.

Feeling suffocated, Maggie ensured that all was as it should be, pocketed her torch and left the house. Peering carefully to make sure that the way was clear, she turned right, back to her car.

In a dingy bar, frequented by an assortment of types, she settled at a small table, drank lager; a drink prevalent, along with beer and the odd G&T, she noted.

Eventually, a man pulled over a stool; sat beside her.

"New here?" he asked.

"Fairly," she replied; aware of the chat-up line but, several lagers in, did not care.

※

What they said; what they did; Maggie cared not to recall, although it lay on her mind as she woke in her car the following morning; head heavy and mind unresponsive. "Coffee," she thought. She uncurled, thankful that no police patrol had noticed her there; stepped out; breathed fresh air; decided to walk back into town as 'hangover therapy'.

She sat with black coffee, nibbled toast prepared by Eileen, the cheerful owner known to a majority of the early morning customers; comforting; a 'home-made' place with half nets at the window.

The bell at the door announced a new customer. Maggie glanced towards it.

Sentinel.

Quickly, she turned, pulled up the collar of her jacket; hoping. She heard Sentinel chat briefly to Eileen, pick up a pre-ordered sandwich and leave.

A sigh of relief. Stupidity on her part. "This is near to where he lives." She had said that she would find him; she must keep her promise; but on her terms.

Chapter Fifteen

Sentinel

Sentinel had seen Maggie; had realised that she did not want to be seen. He respected her need, not to be seen; kept up the pretence with Eileen. Left. Gazed inside, briefly, over the nets. She looked lost; a small huddled figure; fragile.
"Maggie. Who are you?"
Sentinel walked on.

※

Later; after study, after work; he sat in the park beneath a sycamore tree, its foliage rattling against the almost ripe seed pods destined to wing, spin, on the air. Keys. Sycamore keys. Had he such keys, what could he unlock? No space for such thought. Sentinel rose to his feet, retrieved his pack and walked slowly towards what was home, for now.
As he walked, he felt the hurt, Maggie's hurt emanating from within her; as if he was her; it seemed. Her pain becoming his own need; a yearning to ease her pain. Within his own need, he felt desire.
"Only Maggie can close the chasm in my life."

The pain subsided, gradually, as he walked, but he carried the weight of that deep melody; would not let it go.

'If a particle jumps in a random and discontinuous way then it can pass through two slits at the same time'

Shan Gao

Chapter Sixteen

Spindel

This time, this space, is not mine alone. Sentinel is close. I search for Segment in one direction; another. Where is she? Am I on the chosen path?

I feel the pull of Sentinel, along a different way; not the path that I have made my own. I experience anger. My mind twists, contorts; momentarily.

I force myself to run in measured paces. I can outrun Sentinel; be free. I will be free. I can soar; will soar with Segment as my guide.

※

Round a bend in the path, I see a figure ahead. Segment; it must be Segment. My feet spring, leap. There is a shadow beside Segment; not a figure. It has no substance; a shade. I miss a beat in the rhythm of my pace; regain that beat. I sense a shadow at my side; my alter persona, Sentinel.

Do we pursue each other; Sentinel and I? Do we pursue Segment and the shade? Or is it two simultaneous actions? Who is the shade ahead? I recognise the shadow at my side.

※

The path narrows to become a thread leading to a needle with two eyes. Segment and the shade are beyond. It will be impossible to move together; yet we do. I, Spindel, and 'shadow of Sentinel' fuse; pass through both eyes of the needle, together, in an instant; sense the passing, yet do not split. A surge parts us. I am carried on to the place where Segment waits. Sentinel no longer claims my space; nor does the shade hover close to Segment.

※

Exhausted, I fall to the ground. I hear Segment call my name.
"Spindel. Time to move on."
I rise, follow in her wake as a sleepwalker leaving his bed.
"You have been touched, Spindel."
I know by whom; Sentinel; but decline to admit this.
"No."
"Do you wish to change direction; follow another path?"
"No," I lie, yet do not lie; am torn.
Ultimately, my path leads to Sentinel. But not now. This time and space belong to Spindel and Segment. My desire, the symphony.
Segment indicates a fork in the path and we move to the right.
"Stay with me, Segment."
"For now. One day I must return to my own," she reminds me.
"Why?" Although I know the answer, the question is asked.

I, Spindel, desire this time, this space, to be forever.
"Because I am one of many," Segment reminds me.
"Then you will not be missed."
I grasp the words and hurl them as hailstones. Segment turns. Our eyes meet. I witness the hurt within.
"Then you must return," I concede.
"Eventually," she answers.

Chapter Seventeen

Sentinel

A week passed. More. Another. Three. Four. Maggie had not sought him out. Would she? Ever. Never? Sentinel forced himself forward in his study, in small pieces of work to which he was contributing; hardly able to engage with his temporary colleagues. Maggie's deep melody drew him. He held it; would not let go. His own chasm, raw, gaping as a wound and into which he dreaded falling.

Mistakes. Mistakes in his study, small errors in work; not from lack of concentration; his mind cut off thought, tangled ideas. Sentinel sensed that his mind was missing; elsewhere. To grasp at anything, a monumental task; pain in the attempt; unbearable. He made corrections, painstakingly; hours that should have been minutes; determined not to fall short of expectation. He accepted no new work.

The ability to study evaded him; veered off at a tangent. Sentinel watched ability leave the edge of his mind; enter the void left when his mind abandoned him. Not a logical thought but, to him, a reality. His mind had soared; left him to face the chasm on his own.

A sense of being 'outwith' seized him. Sentinel had arrived

where, it seemed, no one else had been. Maggie out of reach; out of touch. Should she search him out, he would not be found. Alone, he trod desolate wastes; expecting to be consumed by chasms of despair.

Eventually, he was told to take a break; that he was not coping; to consider his path; his future. So Sentinel left his room (for use of students only) complete with mural, pulled his coat close to him; protection against the cold; against the vacant space he would enter; where his mind should be. He had been offered a refuge for his break; for a month or so; a journey away. If he could board that train, find the place, he could hibernate until his mind returned; found him.

Not recalling the journey; closing it off as he travelled to minimise an unsafe experience; he arrived at his destination; a bungalow standing alone within a field; for summer use only. A raw wind bit his face. Sentinel pressed forward, key in hand so that it would not follow his mind; become lost.

Winter; cruel, barren of delights, with no redeeming features. Constant wind and howling waves whose crashes of anger were borne by the wind to his ears. A winter at war with itself.

Once inside, with a small fire of logs, left at the side of the hearth, Sentinel allowed himself to sink, huddled, into an old, but comfortable, chair. He stared at the flames; licking; dancing; subsiding to glow with heat.

Food. He had none. Tomorrow would do. There was always tomorrow. Sentinel resisted that route; 'tomorrow'. Exhaustion claimed him and he slept; deeply.

The embers turned to ash.

※

Sentinel bought according to his daily needs and as he was able, from the small shop in the village; a good walk along a minor road. A scarf round his neck and lower face held off the elements and provided some anonymity. He communicated with nods and the odd word when required; the effort exhausting.

Days passed. The relief of each ending. The dread of another beginning. Lost, apart from an awareness of his surroundings; in no particular space. Time, a fog laden blanket that did not lift. Sentinel remained in that place.

Chapter Eighteen

Maggie

Maggie realised that her days at the cottage were coming to an end. She must not outstay her welcome; be discovered. Twice, she had narrowly escaped being sighted by the agent, arriving with prospective buyers. She should complete her task and leave. Or, take the suitcase with her to another location. Maggie did not want to carry her past. Here. Her Dad lived here. Here, she must leave him.

※

During late afternoon of that day, with sufficient daylight left, Maggie retrieved the suitcase from under the stairs. This time, she went up to the bedroom; no need to spread out photographs, nor the slips of paper. Underneath lay the notebook; an 'exercise' book.

Tentatively, Maggie opened the cover, turned to the first page of writing.

※

'Margaret. I need to talk to you but can't. – why did you go? –
it's cruel Margaret – I have Maggie but not you – what could I
do?
I haven't betrayed you
When I saw you drained of life and the baby screaming –
Margaret I wanted to be with you – wherever you had gone –
Not with a squalling infant. Not. NOT with your sister
That's all'

*

'Now it is over!
We have pushed you away – down into the ground – I can't see
you – can't touch you – can't think'

*

'The arrangements are made Margaret
I am to marry Mabel
Why?
If I DON'T she WILL NOT support me – care for Maggie
Can't do it
She WON'T – without marriage'

'Today is the day
HOW CAN I??
Margaret this is OUR day – will marry you – close my eyes to
Mabel – it will look real
IT WON'T BE!!
When we are married I can grieve you forever'

*

'I care for the child Margaret – she is yours – ours – can't bear it – she cheated you of life'

*

'Mabel gloats.
She has won – thinks she has - never will – Margaret - Margaret'

*

'She knows
Margaret – she knows – she never had me – tried to claim me NO – NOT POSSIBLE!!'

*

'Can't stay
Not long now – go – I'll go where we can be together – a quiet place
They both cheated – Mabel cheated me – Maggie cheated you'

*

'Have my things together Margaret – found a cottage – sold shares – a quiet place – just us – at last Margaret'

*

'Here I am Margaret – here – with you – no need to write more – we can talk – feel I have waited forever'

'Will put this in a suitcase with the photos – with the PAPER CHATS – everything
Will do it NOW – then we can look around
Our home Margaret – OUR HOME!'

✵

With these words, the writing ended. Stunned, Maggie sat against the pillow cushioning her from the hard wood of the headboard, unable to move. It had been written in short bursts over time, inconsistently and on odd pages throughout the book; over the years of her growing. That was obvious. And the handwriting changed style slightly, which confirmed the passage of time. It was not dated.

This was Dad. He never was – not truly. Mabel. Mum. She never was. Maggie had never belonged to her parents, Dad and Margaret; was the product of their love only.

Rage. Rage welled to bursting. Maggie grabbed at the pages, ripping, tearing; made shreds of them; destroying something of which she had never been a part.

She tossed the photos onto the bed and chose one. "Why?" she considered. Proof, perhaps, of the parents who abandoned her. The remainder of the photographs she cut, with scissors from the kitchen, deliberately into strips.

Maggie tipped every piece, every scrap, into the open suitcase; snapped it shut. Left, with matches in her pocket, and drove to the shore. She chose a stretch empty of people; laid the case on the stones there; opened the case; struck two, three matches and stood to watch the contents burn. They were rapidly consumed.

She sat beside the scorched case, waiting; stared out to sea; filled her mind with the ocean. When she knew that the suitcase had cooled, Maggie pressed the two halves together as best she could.

"I should have brought string for this," she chastised herself.

Lifting it with both hands, she walked to the edge of the sea; into the sea as far as her calves. Turned to ensure that there was no 'voyeur', raised the case as high as she could and hurled it to the hungry waves.

"Let them devour it in their own time!" she announced.

Satisfied, Maggie waded out, onto the pebbles, up to the larger stones. She did not look back. A sense of desolation came upon her. The stones crunched; her feet squelched in her shoes.

Sentinel. Maggie remembered Sentinel; her promise.

※

Back at the cottage, she gathered together her belongings; checked that all remained as it should; closed the door and walked back to her car, barefoot, with her wet shoes and the house key in her hand. As she drew level with an unkempt patch of land where grasses had grown tall, Maggie threw the duplicate key to lie there; forgotten. The shoes she dropped into a bin beside where she had parked the car. She took her sandals from the car boot and slipped them on; put the backpack into the boot in their place.

She drew the car away from the kerb.

"Sentinel. I must not break my promise. I can't."

※

He was not there; had left some time ago. Maggie asked around. She had to find him.

Chapter Nineteen

Sentinel

One day, as colour left the sky and the wind, never far, prepared to howl into the night, Sentinel heard a car engine and tyres bouncing, scraping their way up the rough drive to the bungalow. He sat, tense, alert, ready to ward off intrusion. The doorbell buzzed for the first time since Sentinel took up residence. He froze. The flap on the letterbox lifted. There was no hallway; the front door opened into the main room. The lights were not on. He remained still; silent.

"Sentinel!"

His name; called through the letterbox.

"Sentinel! Open the door – please."

Maggie. It could not be Maggie. Sentinel could not move.

"Please, Sentinel. It's Maggie. Let me in!"

He stood. Took measured paces to the door; lifted the latch.

"Sentinel."

Maggie pushed against the door. Sentinel laughed within, at his foolishness.

"Of course Maggie," he told himself; only Maggie knew his name.

She burst in.

"Sentinel, it's cold out there. Didn't you know?"

"I didn't realise – that it was you Maggie. And then I did. Sorry."

"Don't be."

Maggie dropped her backpack.

"Tea? Or something. It was a long drive."

"You found me."

"I did, Sentinel. I promised. But only because you had shown me where you were staying. Because no one knew your name, I described you; pretended that I did not know your name, had only met you briefly; that you had lent me something and that I wanted to return it."

"Thank you," he said.

"I promised," she smiled.

※

Snuggled on the couch, they drank tea; ate toast with marmalade; smiled in contentment as children safe and satisfied; grinned conspiratorially; the conspiracy of being together, hidden from the elements.

Sentinel gazed into the fire, to which he had added some logs.

"There are caverns between the logs. In a coal fire they are amazing – blue gases, spitting, hissing."

"I see them, Sentinel. I see the caverns."

"When I was a child, I explored them – in my mind. I conjured wizards, demons and treasure of beauty beyond imagination."

Maggie, curled in a corner of the couch, against a cushion, reached over, touched Sentinel's shoulder; leaned into his responsive arm; laid her head on his chest. He watched as the firelight caught wisps of her hair; highlighted the copper tones.

They sat in silence as dark descended. Drifted into sleep; a breathing space.

※

The numbness in his arm woke Sentinel. He felt a creeping chill invading the room, shivered. The fire lay as ash. Maggie stirred as he attempted to resuscitate his arm.

"Maggie," he whispered. "It's cold now. The fire is out."

"I was so tired. It's a long journey."

"I know. You need to sleep – in a bed. Come with me."

Maggie raised herself, yawned, stretched; sat up and lowered her feet to the floor.

"Lead on!" she half laughed, her voice drowsy with sleep.

She followed Sentinel to one of the doors leading from the room. He opened it.

"In here," he said. "This room looks out to the back. There are low hills several fields away – but you'll see them in the morning."

"Thank you, Sentinel," murmured Maggie as she entered the bedroom.

"Here's your backpack. The bathroom is the door to the left.

Hope you sleep well"

"You, too, Sentinel."

Sentinel closed the door gently, collected the mugs and plates; took them to the kitchen. He felt surreal; were that possible; as if he was a strange object in a foreign place. The evening appeared in his mind as a dream; as if he should check that Maggie had arrived.

He stood in the bathroom brushing his teeth, trying to return the pattern of his thought back to reality.

Too tired for further thought, he opened the door to his own bedroom, crossed to his welcoming bed. Drawing the covers up to ward off the cold of the night, Sentinel closed his eyes; held the promise of tomorrow before him; which would be 'today' when he woke.

※

Following a momentary lapse, when she could not immediately recall her present surroundings, Maggie listened to the soft drips of rain falling incessantly, outside. Desperate to cleanse herself of recent experience, she slid from between the sheets and moved quietly to the door.

Relieved that Sentinel did not appear to be around, Maggie crossed to the front door, turned the key, lifted the latch and stepped out side, pulling the door to. The cold felt exhilarating as she stood in her T-shirt, face tilted to take the force of the drops and allowed herself to become drenched, before being driven indoors by their icy stings.

As she ran across the carpet towards the bathroom, Sentinel appeared, log laden, at the kitchen door, his waterproof dripping, his hair and trousers soaked.

"Maggie!"

"Oh! Sentinel!" And she laughed. "Drowned rats," she told him. "I'm about to run a hot bath. I'll leave the water for you – if you like. I'm clean from the rain, but cold." Maggie shivered involuntarily.

"Please," answered Sentinel. "I'll stack these logs. And discard these." He indicated his wet clothes. "The towels –," but Maggie had shut the door; was running the bath water.

✹

Maggie had cooked breakfast; laid it out on the kitchen table; had turned on the heater to take off the chill; poured tea into mugs.

"What shall we do today, Sentinel?" asked Maggie as they sat down to eat.

Sentinel had not thought beyond the moment; had no plan.

"Do we need to shop? Or can we hibernate until the rain lessens?"

"It's too wet to walk, Maggie."

"My car. I have my car."

"Of course. I had forgotten." As an afterthought, Sentinel added, "Are you staying, Maggie?"

"I think I should," she answered.

The fridge and cupboards were almost bare; the bacon used and only one egg and three tomatoes left. They had obviously eaten the last of the bread the evening before. There was no particular evidence of Sentinel's existence in the bungalow; no work pending, no bits and pieces, nor half read books.

Sentinel looked at Maggie; wondered at her comment; looked down at his empty plate.

"Questions. Can you answer questions, Sentinel?"

"What?" Sentinel did not appear to understand.

"Well. Why are you here? Or, what are you *doing* here?"

"Someone said that I could stay here," was his answer.

"I know," affirmed Maggie. "But that was because you couldn't stay where you were. Something crushed you."

Sentinel, overwhelmed, did not react because he could not say, "It was you, Maggie – you left me for too long." No one could say that of another; without causing pain; remorse. "Maggie is so fragile," his continued thought, "and doesn't know it."

Allowing these thoughts to pass, Sentinel knew his answer and spoke; eventually.

"It all became too much. Study, work, pressure; it builds up until you don't know where you are, don't know what you want to do. Can't do anything."

"But this is temporary – here. You can't stay here forever, Sentinel, hiding from life."

"I'm not," he stated, realising as he spoke that he was doing exactly that. "Can I hide for a while, Maggie?"

Maggie laughed, ran round the table and hugged him from

behind.

"We could both hide," she suggested.

Sentinel turned, surprised.

"If that is what you want to do," he answered.

"Today! Let's hide today!"

Sentinel fought back tears of 'tomorrow'.

Hope: 1

'Hope is the thing with feathers
That perches in the soul,
And sings the tune without the words,
And never stops at all,'

Emily Dickinson

Chapter Twenty

Spindel

Our pathway lies beside a river running fast. Logs bob on the surface; cut logs; escaping their previous confines; some have frayed rope attached.

"We can cross," states Segment.

"Over the logs?" I query.

I, Spindel, watch the logs' haphazard movement; spinning, turning, rolling.

"Perhaps. Or ride them until they beach on the opposite bank."

"Why?"

"The path you have chosen continues on the other side. This was the bridge. If we do not cross now, we may not have another opportunity."

"Do you know where I am going?"

"I know where you are bound, by your choice. I cannot say whether or not you will arrive."

I summon determination; the courage to launch into the current; to cling onto a passing log. Segment is about to leap.

"If we are separated ......" I cry, but my voice is lost to Segment; not a match for the roar of the river.

I leap; and hope. I land, almost but not quite, on a log; cling to a shred of rope and pull, using every fibre of strength within me, until I am spread on the log, my arms wrapped around its girth; as far as they are able. The roar and the rhythm possess me; a cacophony of percussion with a rush of cymbals; marking a dark phrase. My mind is numb; I cannot think; reason.

In a sudden burst I ride high, cresting waves, free of that darkness; a spirit riding the ocean, luminous against a night sky; an ocean backlit by the moon. Exhilarated; free from restraint, borders, boundaries. Careening as if I am a sail set free from its vessel; rise above waves, foam; soar to that night sky.

Before me a glistening path, not of foam; stars or sea pearls? I glide along its direction not caring where it is headed; to the moment, the experience, I hold.

※

In rapture, I behold dazzling light; the vision of that city of glass palaces floats, ablaze with light reflecting light. Shimmering; a mirage. I close my eyes against its intensity, almost impossible to imagine; yet I, Spindel, have it in mind.

※

Prince Parsu and Princess Olmi; she wears a simple crown of purest diamonds, her beauty undiminished by their splendour; enhanced; appear at tall glass doors open to a balcony. Behind them, deep into a ceremonial hall, a towering cake of ice. A star glistens at its pinnacle. It is their wedding feast; an ice dream. Will they become ice as they seal their vows; frozen in time?

※

The dream dissolves. I experience increasing pain; the pain of extreme, penetrating cold. I cannot hold on. I hear a voice; force my eyes to open.

"Spindel. You have arrived."

It is Segment encouraging me onto the bank. I drag my numb form as far as I am able. She clothes me in a web of warmth. I am safe. I have borne both depth and height; rest on neutral soil.

Chapter Twenty One

Maggie

It became obvious to Maggie that she should draw out Sentinel from himself and decided that she should stay; for a while. The report that needed to be completed could be assembled here in loose form and finalised, sent off, when she found adequate Internet access; unless she was mistaken in her assumption that there was no connection, here.

Her initial suggestion, to Sentinel, was to shop for food.

"If we are to hide, Sentinel, we need food. I can't see much in the fridge, nor the cupboards."

"I didn't think. I'm sorry. I wasn't expecting anyone."

"Exactly. But here I am and thinking of lunch already. Let's find coffee. There must be a coffee place somewhere. And is there a harbour? And, if so, is there fresh fish? Questions, Sentinel. Are there answers?"

"I only walked to the small shop and bought bits and pieces. I haven't explored – looked around. Disorientated. I felt disorientated. It was easier not to think, plan. Something like that."

"Well, now we have to. Get ready and I'll turn the car round. You'll come with me?"

"Yes. Yes, I will."

※

Driving through mist and rain, they headed into the village; drove through, to discover that the shop was, indeed, the only one. Maggie followed the road out, heading for the nearest small town. As she drove, she wondered about Sentinel, sitting silently beside her, staring into the mist ahead. Wondered if he would remain in his shell; a reluctant snail. She considered, briefly, what she was doing. Her promise; keeping her promise. That was all she intended to tell herself; shut the door on childhood, who she might be; for now.

Words of a poem tried to push through; words learned in school. She attempted to string them together, but they remained out of reach; persistent though hazy at the back of her mind.

She stopped the car and turned to Sentinel.

"Some words, Sentinel, words of a poem from school – woods and promises – a man on a journey in the snow."

He looked at her, bemused.

"Does it sound familiar to you?"

"Yes," he answered, eventually, and laughed. "I know them. They are from Robert Frost's poem 'Stopping by Woods on a Snowy Evening'."

"It's a beautiful poem, Maggie – poignant."

Sentinel recited the poem.; a favourite that he had committed to memory. Maggie listened intently, shutting out all else.

"The memory just came to me – from school-days, I think. I don't know why."

"You do. It's your promise that's reminded you. Your promise to find me."

Maggie turned away.

"Maggie, you don't have to keep it."

"I do, Sentinel. I keep my promises."

Maggie turned back to him; kissed his forehead, gently.

"For the poem," she said.

"Thank you," he answered.

"My pleasure," she smiled. "Coffee?"

"Yes please."

※

In the town they found a café. Inside, it was warm and steamy from wet customers seeking refuge from the weather.

"Gingerbread men! I see gingerbread men, Sentinel! Let's begin our adventure with gingerbread men."

"Are we having an adventure?"

"I think so. We are both doing something different – something we don't know."

"Yes. I am."

"Me too, Sentinel. Gingerbread men then!"

They drank coffee and nibbled gingerbread men, not needing to talk; just occasional smiles.

"Now, a list, Sentinel," announced Maggie, as she finished her coffee, picked up the paper serviette that she had not used and took a pen from her pocket. She listed necessities, treats that they should hunt for and a question mark for surprise purchases.

"That's an odd way to make a list, Maggie."

"It's an adventure, Sentinel. There must be surprises."

Leaving the warmth of the café, they made their way up the town's High Street, pleased that the rain had decreased to a misty drizzle. Maggie linked her arm into Sentinel's. The adventure had begun.

※

Back at the bungalow, Maggie stored the provisions while Sentinel arranged their wet outdoor clothes over the kitchen chairs.

"Are there games here?" Maggie turned to Sentinel.

"Yes. In a cupboard."

"Well ….."

"I'll get one out – bring it in here."

"Or, we could play it in there – on the coffee table."

"Right. I'll light a fire first."

Maggie carried plates of snacks and two glasses of wine through from the kitchen. An embryo fire lay in the hearth, gaining strength. Sentinel had laid out the game at one end of the coffee table. She knelt down beside him.

"Snakes and ladders!" she exclaimed. "Like life," she added.

"Perhaps. Perhaps not," said Sentinel.

The snacks were gone, the game ended. Sentinel had won. Maggie jumped onto the couch and curled in a corner.

"Fun. I had fun."

Sentinel joined her.

"We are like children," he mused.

"No. No, don't say that, Sentinel."

She had spoken sharply; alarmed Sentinel. He was retreating.

"Sentinel. Sentinel, don't go away, into your snail shell. Stay here, " she pleaded.

He looked uncertain. Maggie could hardly bear it. "He is such a beautiful person." She moved closer; repeated aloud, "Don't. Please don't."

She looked at him directly until she could not see through the tears blinding her vision.

"Maggie."

Maggie felt Sentinel holding her closely, stroking her hair, rocking her; a child in its mother's arms. Inconsolable; it was safe to be inconsolable.

At last, her adventure had begun.

Chapter Twenty Two

Sentinel

"Maggie. Maggie."

Sentinel sensed grief. "She is grieving." He did not consider for whom or what she grieved; accepted Maggie's grief.

How long they sat, he could not recall. Eventually, she moved away; to the bathroom to regain composure. The rain had stopped. A watery sun filtered sparse rays.

"Let's walk, Sentinel," announced Maggie as she reappeared. "Where can we go?"

"Down to the shore?" he ventured.

Maggie laughed.

"Shores seem to belong to us," surmised Sentinel. "We could walk inland – towards the hills."

"No. The shore is fine. The sea should be rough – pounding waves – exciting."

They set off.

"I love the music of the sea, Maggie. The quiet ripples of calm and the crashing movement of storm tossed days."

"The sea is restless, Sentinel – always on the move."

"Is that like you, Maggie?" Asked Sentinel.

"No. I have no rhythm guiding me – just one day and then the next."

When they reached the shore, Sentinel gazed out to sea.

"I would like a rhythm, Maggie. I think that there is a rhythm within me, but it has not been set free."

"Mine is lost, Sentinel. Lost."

"Maggie, don't say that!"

He grasped her firmly, pulled her towards him; held her tight.

"Maggie." He released a hand to stroke her hair. "Feel safe somewhere."

"You too, Sentinel."

And he knew it for the truth.

"Are we lost?" he asked.

"Perhaps, " she answered.

"You and I – together –"

"Don't say it, Sentinel! Don't say it! Not now. Not yet. Perhaps never."

"You are precious," he told her; climbing down from the impulse of his passion for Maggie.

But he kissed her. "We are two souls," his thought as he released her. "Two souls who long for something that is not – as yet."

She stroked his nose; broke the spell.

"Time to move on – time for us to be waves in continuous motion."

Sentinel looked at the seaweed tossed in loose patterns on the shore.

"Let me tell you a story," he began, remaining still.

Maggie did not respond. His arm moved lightly to rest around her waist.

"This seaweed. These patterns, haphazard as they are, mark the preparation for a queen to arrive. Out there, Maggie, far out, are Wogles, creatures of the sea. They wait for their queen. When there are storms, they ride them to the shore, lay garlands of seaweed to welcome her return."

Maggie listened, amused.

"And does she?" she asked.

"Not yet," he replied, "but they do not give up hope. One day – one day, she will return and they will take her with them, out as far as they go – to where a bower on the sea bed awaits her presence. And as she sleeps, they will sing."

"What are they singing? Sea shanties?"

"No, Maggie. They sing lullabies, play sonatas using fibres and shells, whatever lies there – make melodies. And she smiles in her sleep – content – glad to have returned."

"How do you know?" laughed Maggie.

"Because. Because I feel it here, within. I know that that is how the story goes – eventually."

Maggie nuzzled her head into his coat.

"That is a fantasy."

"Perhaps," he answered.

They continued to walk, listening to their steps crush the wet sand, feeling the softness of the dying wind; catching the last rays of a lowering sun.

✵

Refreshed, they arrived back at the bungalow, discarded their coats and drew the curtains against the cold approach of night.

"Rekindle the fire, Sentinel. I'll see what we can make from the bounty we collected this morning. Shall we cook together?"

※

"That was fun. Maggie."

Sentinel lay back on the couch, relaxed.

The meal over, the washing and drying done and the day drawing to a close; he knew that 'today' was to continue. Tomorrow would inevitably become 'today' as would each day following. For how long? Sentinel had no desire to know. Maggie joined him.

"Well?"

"Well what?"

"How is it going – our adventure, our hiding away?"

"Hmm. What do I think? It is a beginning, Maggie, perhaps not of hiding as I had supposed, but the beginning of a beginning."

"Very profound, Sentinel," mocked Maggie and Sentinel smiled, content that he could; without fear.

"Can we ask questions, Maggie?"

"No. Not today."

Sentinel wondered about tomorrow; when it became 'today'.

"Sleepy?" he enquired.

"Sleepy," she nodded. " I think I'll go to bed."

Maggie padded across to her room.

"Goodnight, Sentinel," she called from the doorway.

"Goodnight," he replied.

Sitting in the half light from the fire, Sentinel knew that he could be himself; the self of his childhood; the self that he knew. He watched the embers glow and fade and ash fall silently.

※

Over breakfast the following day; their second 'today' but the third in total; Sentinel decided to ask Maggie a question, but not in question form.

"Tell me something, Maggie. Tell me something I need to know."

Putting aside her toast, Maggie considered before she answered.

"If I told you that I am looking for something that I lost, can you accept that?"

A sadness passed over Sentinel; Maggie had lost a part of herself. To lose a part of oneself; inconceivable to Sentinel. "I have claimed myself. I may be lost but, it is I who am lost. At times I am parted from myself, but my 'self' is never lost," ran his thoughts.

"I do not want to accept it, Maggie, because it is a part of yourself that is lost and not some thing," he told her.

He watched as Maggie realised the extent of his understanding. She bit on her toast and drank tea in silence.

"Tell me when I need to know," he advised, not wanting to push Maggie further, and took command of 'today'.

"I can drive us up the coast to discover a wild place, Maggie.

Will you let me drive?"

He took note of a thankful glance, followed by a grin as she pushed back her chair to take her cup and plate to the sink.

"Of course," she answered looking at him, over her shoulder.

"I meant it, Maggie."

"I know. Make me a picnic while I get ready, Sentinel. Picnics are treats and a surprise picnic – well, I can hardly wait to eat it!"

She laughed and ran from the kitchen.

Sentinel's enthusiasm and imagination inspired him as to what would surprise Maggie; what would be a treat.

"Coming, ready or not!" he heard Maggie call, in fun, after some twenty minutes or so; as if it was a game of 'hide and seek'.

"Ah, but I *am* ready," he called back. "You shall have your surprise but, first, pass me the car keys. I'm putting your picnic in the boot and there it stays until we are ready to eat."

He heard a clatter of keys land on the wood of the floor outside her door, pocketed them and headed for the front door carrying a cardboard box which contained the picnic.

※

Sentinel had not driven in some time and was not sure if he should be driving Maggie's car, but the roads and lanes were almost devoid of vehicles. The elation he felt, at having suggested the outing and that he be the driver, lifted his level of confidence. He had begun to slide from what Maggie called his 'snail shell'.

'Every body perseveres in its state of being at rest or of moving uniformly forward except insofar as it is compelled to change its state by forces impressed'

Sir Isaac Newton

Chapter Twenty Three

Spindel

A movement ends; another is to begin. Radiance emanates from Segment as she hovers beside me; or so it seems in my semi conscious state. Do I continue along this way? Can I, Spindel, countenance more pain. My eyes open; I look around. This landscape reveals no redeeming feature; an interval. There is no music in this interval; space only. Am I to renege on my search or, is it possible to seek and find?

As I sit, Segment plucks occasional notes from a harp string. The sound of a harp is what I, Spindel, hear and there is no presence other than Segment and Spindel in this place. I turn my head to watch her play.

"Your harp. Where is your harp?" I ask, not able to see the instrument.

"I have no harp, Spindel."

"You were playing, plucking a string, creating notes."

"I smoothed my garment, Spindel, to remove dust."

There is no harp; yet a harp enticed me from sombre thoughts that would not lead to where I intend to go. The symphony lies ahead; not in any other direction. The notes perceived in my mind, the beginning of a movement for strings; delicate, shimmering sound, balancing flight of fancy against the warmth of assurance. I take them with me.

"I shall continue," I, Spindel, say and rise with intention.

Segment smiles, helps me to the path, sings encouragement that holds no words; captures the lucidity of sound.

On, into the night we travel; Segment as a firefly lighting the night; a flitting star held close to the ground by gravity. And, in the galaxy above, reflected light of stars mimic, twinkle; stand sentinel, marking a pathway through space. A step too far for us, but I sense a longing to rise; to rise into that space; eternity maybe. Segment and Spindel together; no longer separate entities.

"Spindel. Breathe the scents of night," urges Segment.

We pause; breathe in unison an elixir which draws us from ourselves. We glide along the perfumed trail, around and around, arms entwined to unite our bodies; spirits. A waltz. Perhaps a waltz. I cannot be certain. It is enchantment and I desire it to have no end.

Morning breathes on us as the sun rises. We have danced the night through; arrived at the next phrase.

Segment understands my mission. Segment, my muse, will initiate the symphony and, in so doing, will return to her own. I know this. I shall bring her forward. It is my rôle to lead; conduct her. I cannot force; must be diligent, patient; nurture Segment. And if I do not? The symphony is lost.

This day is pivotal.

Chapter Twenty Four

Sentinel

Sun warmed his face through the car windscreen. Colours of autumn shone in the dazzling light; vibrant, clear. Sentinel held the glow.

"Autumn. Blue skies. What a combination!" Maggie exclaimed.

"I would love to paint those colours, Maggie, but I work better in pencil."

"Rust. The colour of decay, decomposition, but alluring all the same."

"I never thought of it in that sense – just of colour combinations – vivid contrasts."

Sentinel lapsed into contented silence. Maggie looked relaxed.

Eventually, the road became a lane and the car bumped along. They laughed as they covered the rough terrain until they could go no further.

"Here we are!" he announced.

"Looks like it, Sentinel."

Sentinel opened the door, let in autumn air spiced with sea salt; breathed deeply. He walked round to open Maggie's door.

"A gentleman!" smiled Maggie.

"Of course," Sentinel smiled back.

They stretched their limbs and stood, looking out to the horizon. Wind from the sea pushed against them. Maggie's hair streamed; freely. Sentinel hugged her to him. She snuggled against him, her face turned away from the wind. His arm remained around her shoulders. On the deep blue surface of the sea waves danced, frolicked.

"The sea is at play," decided Maggie.

"So it is," answered Sentinel.

"Today, we can play, too, Sentinel."

He squeezed Maggie gently in affirmation. 'Today', he thought. 'How long will 'today' last?' His hope was that it would last forever; as certain and lasting as the sea.

He dropped his arm.

"You can collect your picnic, now, Maggie. You choose where we shall eat."

Maggie ran to the car boot; opened it.

"It's in a box!"

"Indeed," he replied. "A box full of surprises."

He lifted it from the boot.

"Lead the way, Maggie!"

She made her way to the shore. A layer of pebbles and stones covered the sand at the top of the beach, where boulders and rocks lay strewn. The low tide exposed sand and shells leading to the water's edge. A cool breeze blew in.

"Here! Here!" Maggie indicated a boulder where they could sit sheltered, in part, from the breeze and warmed by the sun.

"Perfect," agreed Sentinel and put down the picnic box.

Sentinel watched Maggie excitedly open up the top. There, he had placed a light rug.

"To sit on," was her verdict.

Maggie laid it on the ground. She delved into the box, bringing out one surprise package after another, each in a different coloured wrapping; from his 'art store'.

"A rainbow picnic! How wonderful," she smiled.

Sentinel saw joy spread from within, revealed in her face. "At last," he thought, "Maggie has felt joy touch her." It was no longer desire but love that filled him. Overwhelmed, he turned to the sea. He did not want Maggie to witness the emotion he forced himself to contain.

He turned back to see Maggie unwrapping the small food parcels.

"Come on, Sentinel!" she called. "Come and eat!"

※

"That was amazing Sentinel," Maggie pronounced as they sat back against the boulder; full, contented.

"Joy – yes, it was a joy to eat surprise after surprise. How could you make it so special?"

"Because I love you," he yearned to say.

"Because you are special. Maggie," he said.

"Flattery, Sentinel!" Maggie laughed.

"I am losing her again," he realised; held down panic.

"No. I wanted to show you that you *are* a special person.

Sometimes, I think that you don't know it."

He could see that Maggie had become unsure; defensive.

"Don't think about it, now, Maggie. This is 'today'. This time is for us – just for us. True?"

Maggie had let go of her darker thoughts; he could see her letting go. She shook her head as if to rid herself of them altogether.

"True, Sentinel."

She leaned against him and they rested. Maggie dozed. Sentinel stared out at the shoreline, the sea, the sky touching it at the horizon. He saw himself and Maggie touch in that seamless way; 'today'.

Maggie roused herself as a cloud slid across the sun; shivered.

"It's colder, now."

Sentinel knelt, took her by the shoulders.

"Let's walk, then."

He helped her to her feet and she set off, leading the way; hugging her body with her arms, striding towards the shoreline. Sentinel watched as he followed in her wake.

Suddenly, Maggie flung open her arms, tilted her head to the sky; shook it vigorously and began to dance, following the wind and the rhythm of spume crested waves. Sentinel stopped; stood mesmerised. His whole being ached. He longed to be a part of that dance; that movement; that rhythm. The wild movement subsided; became, for him, a melody full of grace; sorrow; and lifted again to soar, blend effortlessly with the elements; as if Maggie would rise and disappear.

He ran towards her. She paused, took him with her to move as one, conducted by the ocean; their combined sound blown to the rim of the sky.

Exhausted, they fell onto the sand, laughing; elated.

"You are ….," began Sentinel.

She pressed her fingers to his lips, preventing more. They lay in silence until the wind beat more strongly and with bite.

Sentinel sat up.

"Come on," he said, affectionately stroking wisps of hair from her face.

"Time to go."

Maggie clasped him tightly. He felt the warmth of her tears touch his neck; controlled his breathing to stifle sobs welling within. As these subsided, he kissed her hair.

"Beautiful, Maggie. Your hair is beautiful."

But it was Maggie who held the beauty; the entirety of Maggie. 'Today'. Today surpassed all other days before it; almost his hopes, his dreams.

Maggie pulled free; picked up a pebble.

"Take a pebble, Sentinel. Tonight we can tell stories – pebble stories."

Intrigued, Sentinel chose one lying near; slipped it into his pocket.

They stood and made their way pack to the picnic. As they packed away what was left, Sentinel panicked. "We are packing 'today'." In sadness, he turned away, looking at shell patterns on the sand. His eye caught a mussel shell split open, but intact; the fragile halves delicately joined. He picked it up; dusted off the sand. Taking a serviette, he wrapped it carefully. Maggie knelt, folding the rug; had not noticed. Sentinel placed the shell in his pocket, hoping that it would survive the journey.

※

At the car, they looked back and cuddled briefly before settling into their seats. Sentinel started the engine, reversed; set off, leaving 'today' behind.

Chapter Twenty Five

Maggie

That evening, they sat on the floor in front of the fire, its light reflected in their glasses as they drank.

"Where did you find this, Maggie?"

"At the back of the cupboard. We can replace it if it's not yours."

Maggie omitted to say that she had brought the wine; had taken it from her car and stowed it in a cupboard in her room.

"Mmm." Sentinel smiled as he drank.

Maggie scrambled to her feet, leaving her glass on the floor.

"Pebbles. Time for pebble stories."

She ran to her room to retrieve her pebble.

"Find yours, Sentinel!" she called out to him.

"It's here – in my pocket!" he called back.

Maggie reappeared.

"Let's make ourselves comfortable."

She pulled the seat cushion from the couch, so that they could remain on the floor and placed other cushions against the couch, so that they could lean back.

"We could have sat on the couch."

"No, Sentinel. The floor is the right place to be. Bring the glasses."

Sentinel complied. Maggie watched him. There was so much he did not know, could not know; even that she had been considered a thief. Maggie felt the pebble in her hand; conjured in her mind that day at school; odd that it had made its mark, directed her future. She had become a geologist; in defiance, or as a defence? She could not decide which; maybe neither. And, perhaps she was a thief. The pebble in her hand did not belong there, but on a beach. Samples. She had stolen samples from the earth for work purposes. She could well be a thief. Even her father considered her so; she had stolen her mother's life in her own birth.

Sentinel stared at her. "Did he know? No. He was waiting for the stories to begin."

"You go first, Sentinel," she said as she sat down.

"You first, Maggie," he insisted.

Her pebble was patterned with streaks of quartz and sedimentary rock; this knowledge a part of her trade; work. She fingered the smoothness; contemplated its journey.

Maggie told the story of its beginning – one of many broken pieces from a smashed rock. How, licked by the sea, it had tumbled and travelled, seeking its destiny. As it travelled, its inner qualities had emerged; the streaks and veins that were its true self.

"Now," she concluded, "it has been plucked from its environment to stand alone – perhaps. You may return it, Sentinel, to continue its journey. Or, you can keep it."

She stood, walked to the mantelpiece and placed it there. She could sense that Sentinel felt unsure of what to think; what to take from the tale. This could be a dangerous game; she knew from past experience.

"Your turn," she told him and sat back to listen.

Sentinel began. His white pebble glowed; white; almost imperceptible, grey veins scribbled over it.

"This is not how this pebble started out. It, too, was rough. It had no hope, no aspiration – allowed itself to travel, relentlessly bruised by the turmoil of a raging sea and the pressure of other stones, pebbles. There are no mirrors in the sea. Reflections bounce off the surface of the sea – avoid the seabed – being light, not darkness. Years passed. The pebble travelled wherever the sea took it."

Maggie noticed that he looked intently at her all the while he spoke.

"Eventually, it washed up on the shore where I discovered it, today. It had become smooth, almost transparent, showing what it could become ….. if it was allowed to travel on."

Sentinel reached across; placed the pebble in her hand.

"For you, Maggie," he said. "A reminder of today."

She took the pebble; looked directly into his eyes. They drew her in; her whole being. She struggled to salvage something for herself, but could not. He laid her gently down and she allowed him her whole self, because she wanted, needed to.

Firelight and the warmth of the room bathed them. The smoothness of their bodies touching, holding, moving in harmony; as breathing pebbles pressed together; to an ecstatic, crescendo; a suspended pause; this moment, this silence, shared forever.

※

The following morning, they moved as one, preparing breakfast, enjoying each other's proximity.
"Let's eat, then."
Maggie sat. Sentinel poured tea and joined her; carried the cups to the table. She did not refer to last night; nor did he. Sun shone through the window over the sink. They lingered over the tea. Maggie contemplated her thoughts, attempting to understand where she stood; could not. The inner longing vied with her need to 'cut free'; always to be beholden only to herself; emotionally unattached. She looked across at Sentinel with a gentleness that felt strange, but oddly comforting. "Perhaps I could settle – eventually." There had to be 'eventually'. She could not permit 'now'.

She saw Sentinel place one of the picnic serviettes on the table. He had taken it from his pocket. Carefully, he unfolded it to reveal a mussel shell; its halves still joined; exact matches.
"The symmetry of nature," she mused.
"I found it on the beach."
"It's so delicate – precious treasure from the sea," she smiled, thinking of him bringing it back the two tenuously connected halves, without damaging them; his care for their fragility.
"I," he began, "I thought of us."

Maggie frowned; puzzled.

"They are us," he continued. "We belong together, however precarious the connection."

He reached across the table to touch her hand.

Maggie recoiled. She jumped up, pushing back her chair; saw Sentinel's look of horror.

"Maggie!"

"I have to go," she told him.

She did have to go; had not wanted to tell him; had wanted to stay. This had focussed her attention on reality; broke the spell.

Devastation drawn on Sentinel's face showed her what she had done. She had stolen a part of him; felt devastated herself, forced it inwards; begging it not to show. In that instant, she knew. "I am a thief." Dread; the knowledge of her unworthiness; surged over her. She ran to her room, bundled her belongings as best she could; crossed to the front door and out to her car.

Sentinel stood; did not speak; watched.

She closed the car door, but wound down the window.

"Bye!" she called, softly.

Sentinel had followed her.

"Maggie," he said. His eyes searched hers, intently; as if seeking her soul. She saw him struggle to control his emotion.

"Maggie. One promise. Promise me, Maggie, that you will find me again – when you need to. Send an address. I won't follow you - come looking. But, I need to know where you might be – in case."

"In case what?" thought Maggie, already steeled for her

departure.

"A postcard?"

"That's fine, Maggie."

She turned the key. The engine revved. Maggie bumped towards the road; "taking the route of a thief - a robber". She looked back as she headed the car away. Sentinel was no longer there.

'Time is defined so that motion looks simple'

John Archibald Wheeler

Chapter Twenty Six

Spindel

That day, as all days, ended; sped towards evening. The setting sun threaded gold and red across the sky; deepening to rich purple before night revealed its intention; drew out the colour.

I, Spindel, sat apart from Segment who, tired by our journey, slept, curled on a bank of moss. As the night sky unfolded; set out its treasure; I heard chimes; glass chimes rippling, tinkling; peppering the air with pure notes, cascading as a small fall of water hidden from view. If stars cascaded so, sleep would come sweet and clear to all who heard their music.

My mind wandered to falls of snow; empirical, their silence; the sound of silence. Silence; an absence of sound, yet not so as absence composes in its own right; can be claimed by those who dare address its validity. If I, Spindel, were to search for comparison, my answer would be that it is akin to holiness; immeasurable.

Snow falls; stars chime; the breath of silence breathes on me. I rise, as in a sequence of repeats, to the skies; to those palaces of glass; to the tale of Prince Parsu, as it was imparted to me. I, Spindel, rise to face joy or pain, alone; separated from Sentinel; my anchor; my weight.

Their wedding feast has ended. The palace, at this time, one simple palace that stands alone. Prince Parsu, and his Princess Olmi, sleep. No. Parsu sleeps. Olmi lies still, her eyes open wide. A beautifully woven rug covers them. It is woven with the colours of a rainbow; at times white as those colours merge; become light.

I, Spindel, cannot stare as they lie there. My glance takes in the wild fear in Olmi's eyes; the fear of entrapment. I realise this fear; turn away; want no part of it. I must release this image; return. Incalculable heights contain foreboding. I have no desire to achieve the point of no return.

The ground is as soft as my mind imagines. Sleep calls and I move towards Segment; crouch and curl alongside her. We lie as a single shape; secure until morning.

※

We rise. The new day is misted over. Tentatively, we feel our way, shivering from dew fall during the night, which causes our garments to cling coldly to us.

"There will be a parting of the way."
As Segment speaks, her words lie flat in the mist.
"We must part?" This a question I ask.
"Part – no," she answers, "but we must follow parallel paths. Although you will not see me, you will sense my presence."
"When?" Another question.
"As the mist rises and we can see clearly the paths to be taken."

"Would that this mist last forever," I whisper to myself. I can bear cold and clinging wetness, but to part from Segment, travel alone, I feel is beyond my capability.

"You will not be alone, Spindel."

Segment speaks as if she has read my thought.

"You will know that I am there, but in a different form."

She places this suggestion in my mind.

"I shall carry your image with me."

"Yes. Do that, Spindel."

"I will."

We continue, taking slow steps. My thoughts envelope me as a blanket of security. When I break free of them, lift the blanket to breathe more easily, I see that the day is bright and clear; strongly portrayed in blue with no cloud in sight. Do I hold cloud within, is my consideration; perhaps a truth.

Ahead, the way divides; an upper and a lower path.

"I shall go down, Spindel," Segment tells me. "You take the higher path. It is strewn with boulders. The stones are hard on a soft foot. Pass carefully and do not allow pain to prevail."

I feel Segment take my thoughts gently, with a sweep of her arms. She appears to fold and bundle them into a bag she carries. Sitting the bag on the ground, Segment cups my face in her hands and kisses my nose, lightly; steps back, picks up her bag and turns to the path that is to be hers.

"Walk strongly towards yourself, Spindel," she advises. "Persevere."

She leaves me.

I, Spindel, turn to the left fork, towards the higher way. Already, it looks bleak. The voice of Segment echoes in my mind; a cymbal clash and its reverberation. Ahead; the agony that I must endure.

Chapter Twenty Seven

Sentinel

Inside the bungalow, Sentinel sank to the floor in a primal position and howled; unable to tear himself from his instinct.

His howls ran their course and he staggered to his feet; stumbled to the kitchen for water and sat heavily on a kitchen chair. He drank; refilled his glass and drank more. Holding his head in his hands, he allowed despondency to begin its descent; until an image of Maggie filled his mind. With it came the realisation of his knowledge; the knowledge that Maggie needed him; now and always. That she did not, herself, know this, or that she could not admit it, he was unable to decide; left it in abeyance.

The water refreshed Sentinel. He splashed his face at the sink tap; denied despondency its hold on him. Walking back to the room, he permitted their 'today' to calm and heal, temporarily, the gaping hole; the place from which Maggie had been wrenched. He had no doubt that the wound would reopen; that his soul would cry out with emptiness; longing.

※

The following morning, Sentinel began to plan. He could not

hide there forever; was no longer a child in a garden haven. His childhood was safe; intact; a reassurance that he would take into his future. No longer did he need to revisit; twist time back on itself.

He would return to work; to study; think forwards. Today, he intended to tidy; wash and clean. Tomorrow, he would head back to return the bungalow key to its owner; presuming that a train ran on that day. Gone the terror of tomorrow; tomorrow now a hope. He focussed on the practicalities of today.

※

A knock on the door of the colleague's home; a wait; the door opening.

"The key," blurted Sentinel. "I am returning the key. Time at the bungalow was what I needed – space to think. Thank you for your kindness, Peter."

"Not at all. Funny that you should turn up, though. I'm selling the place. Too far away. Too remote. No one wants to holiday there any more."

"Oh," Sentinel stood, stunned.

"Just thought that I would mention it – in case you came across anyone interested in buying."

"No. Not at the moment," answered Sentinel, but knew that he was that person; did not know how to voice it without emotion.

"Thank you," he repeated.

"See you at work then."

"Soon. Yes," answered Sentinel.

"Must go. Guests inside."

Peter indicated the hallway.

"Of course."

Sentinel walked down the drive to the gate.

※

That night, in a room in a 'B&B', his mind crowded with thoughts; raced with possibilities; but to no conclusion. He refocussed on practicalities; work; where to live. There was time and space to resolve those other issues during the following days.

Taking a drawing pad and pencils from his belongings, Sentinel began to draw. His mind and hand created strokes, shades, solid forms; soft evaporating mists with a 'B' pencil. Satisfied with the result; suspended shapes that somehow sounded their own melody on the page; he felt calm; ready to sleep.

※

Back at work, several days later, Sentinel had been engaged to complete a planning assignment abandoned by a cartographer who had decided to travel the world. Whether he had been inspired by maps and plans, or fired with a desire to escape the two dimensional world of his work, no one in the office knew. His exit had been sudden and inconvenient, but provided a slot into which Sentinel conveniently fitted.

Although not comfortable back within the confines of a drawing office, Sentinel concentrated on the task in hand to the exclusion of all else. He still resided at the 'B&B', unsure of his next step. This uncertainty being a result of Peter's announcement that he intended to sell the bungalow. In his mind, it was where he and Maggie belonged and he found it hard to bear thoughts of others trespassing there.

Work over, Sentinel sat in a park located nearby; leaves, in autumnal tones of orange and yellow, lay as patchwork on well kept grass. "Until the gardeners see them," he mused. "Beauty held in the sadness of their demise." He dwelt on the thought; that of beauty in death; tore himself from that pain, his need being life and love. Sentinel decided to check his post office box for mail that could have arrived during the period of his absence.

Not much; apart from an envelope addressed in his mother's handwriting; odd. She was not one to communicate. It had to be informative. Yes. It was. An elderly neighbour had died. Alice. Sentinel had known Alice all his life. She had always shown him kindness; encouraged him. He smiled in affectionate memory; glad, as his mother mentioned that she did not suffer; had passed away peacefully in her old age. Particular memories flooded back; consumed Sentinel. Tears of remembrance filled his eyes. He blinked them back.

There was a second page. He turned to it. Alice had remembered him, his mother wrote, though 'why' she could not imagine; had left a small legacy. Sentinel shook his head. She had no need. Memories of her were a legacy.

※

The following day, Sentinel phoned his mother; listened to her babble of 'almost indignation' that he was to benefit. He asked, what did he need to know; do; did not wish to appear avaricious as it was not in his nature. His mother gave him a phone number; that of Alice's solicitor; hoped that he would be happy with his legacy as that was all that he would get. He did not wish to hear more and carefully brought the conversation to an end.

He sat folding and unfolding the paper on which he had scribbled the number; made a paper aeroplane of it and shot it across the room. He walked to the small window and gazed out. In a few months, the year would draw to a close leaving a vacuum for a new one to begin. Sentinel smiled wryly. 'Today' would be left behind; only 'tomorrow' could become a hope. He crossed to where the paper had fallen; retrieved it; dialled the number.

As he waited, he recalled Alice presenting him with pencils; drawing books; for what was in his mind. "She has probably left me a year's supply of coloured pencils."

A voice; that of the solicitor's secretary. Sentinel explained his business, giving his birth name as verification. As he did so, it came back to him; his name; Sentinel. It was Alice who brought it to him. He could see her standing at the garden gate; leaning on it. He curled, crumpled, on the other side; nursing a graze on his knee; trying not to cry.

'Sentinel,' she had said. 'That is your name. You will be strong – stand firm and be trustworthy. You will be a guardian. Never mind me, though,' Alice had laughed. 'Ramblings of an old woman.'

The words came back to him; clearly. He had not understood, but had liked the name; had taken it. Perhaps he had understood; had been too young to realise.

"Pardon?"

The secretary repeated that he was to come to the office; gave him the address. Sentinel wrote it on the back of the piece of paper on which the phone number was written; arranged a time, two days ahead; thanked her. The call ended.

"Alice. Alice. Thank you for giving me my name." He spoke out into the autumn air; had opened the sash window to let it in. Again, he smiled, thinking of pencils; perhaps a drawing book. He could think no further; only of kindness; that of Alice and her quiet nurturing during his childhood; the knowledge that no one else had been aware of this. He could not imagine how she had known that that person was within; Sentinel; himself.

A night to sleep soundly; in peace; at a place from which 'tomorrow' could begin.

※

The day had come; that in which he was to learn of his legacy. It was an amber day; glowing with autumn gold. He stood outside the building and looked up. The office was on the second floor; the solicitor's name across a window. Sentinel rang; was admitted; made his way up.

He listened carefully to the formalities; almost laughed when the solicitor produced a small box.

"These are for you."

He pushed the box across his desk.

"Thank you."

Sentinel rose to leave.

"No, no! Sit down, please. There is more. A letter which Alice – do you mind if I speak of her informally? I knew her well."

Sentinel could see that he held great affection for Alice.

"Of course not. I only knew her as Alice. I was young and surnames were not an issue."

"True," agreed the solicitor; a Mr. Greyling. He passed the letter to Sentinel.

Alice had not revealed his name. It remained a secret between them. Quietly, he read Alice's words. She explained how she felt that he had great worth but that life would not be easy for him; continued to say that she felt that he would need a refuge; a shelter; at some point in his life. For this reason, she had decided to bequeath him enough for that purpose.

Sentinel could not see through the tears coursing his cheeks, dropping onto the page. Mr. Greyling reached across and gently took the letter in his hand.

"You will want to keep this," he offered as an explanation for his action; passed a box of tissues.

"Thank you."

Sentinel composed himself.

"The shock," he mumbled.

"Quite," answered Mr. Greyling. "Take your time."

"Sorry."

Sentinel sat straight and smiled across the desk.

"If you're ready," ventured the solicitor.

"Yes."

"This legacy is to be released to you when you have found where you wish to live. There will be no actual cash – except for legal fees. Come back to me when you have found somewhere and we can discuss it."

Sentinel nodded in assent.

"I will," he added.

"I presume that you do not own a home as there was no address at which I could reach you – apart from your mother's."

"No, I do not own a home."

"Do you live with your mother?"

"No." Sentinel spoke, he felt, a fraction too abruptly. "No," he modified, "I rent. At the moment, I am between places and am in bed and breakfast accommodation – temporarily."

"Alice was a wise lady," Mr. Greyling told Sentinel. "Very astute, too." He waited a moment. "I think that she was looking out for you, if you don't mind my saying."

"No. No, I don't. And thank you. I appreciate your thoughts."

And for Maggie, too, Sentinel knew.

"Well, that's about it."

Mr. Greyling stood and extended his hand. Sentinel stood.

"Of course."

He shook Mr. Greyling's hand.

"Don't forget your box!"

"No."

Sentinel picked up the box.

"Pencils, I think," smiled Mr. Greyling.

"I thought so," answered Sentinel.

✵

Outside in the street, Sentinel considered himself in a surreal situation; could not think; felt desperate to shout out, "Maggie! Maggie! We can go home!" But he had promised not to follow her. He recalled Frost's lines reiterating the need to fulfil his promises, no matter how far he must travel before he could sleep.

The repeat of the final line; an echo; urging the traveller (or himself) on, was of the essence to Sentinel; his time of waiting a distance to be endured.

Chapter Twenty Eight

Maggie

Maggie had been back some two or three days, catching up on a statistical project requiring completion, scanning emails and ignored messages to see what needed attention; what could be discarded.

The journey back had been horrendous. Relentlessly pursuing the road 'home'; not that she considered anywhere her home but her 'place of being' at any given time. "Did that apply to the time she spent with Sentinel – the bungalow?" She switched off the thought, knowing that it belonged in a category of its own; not wanting to dwell on this.

"Goodness! Is that the time?" She had a meeting to attend. Grabbing necessary material and hastily changing into appropriate clothing, "No need to look a complete mess," she told herself, Maggie slammed the door, left the flat and ran to her car.

※

That evening, fully realising that she had, fortunately, secured a place on the expedition, Maggie looked around the flat. She would be absent for some months, depending on how long it took to gather data, and must concentrate on putting things in order.

Over the following few days, Maggie prepared. Her completed project lay ready for submission; bills had been paid to date and she had no need to inform anyone of her whereabouts; that she would be overseas. "Who would want to know?" Sentinel pushed his way into her mind. "Why should I tell him? He doesn't know where I am anyway." She had not sent a postcard with an address, so it could wait for her return.

The nonchalance with which she dealt with the matter belied her feelings; feelings that bothered her. She pushed them away. "Do I really have to bury you, too, Sentinel, or will you rest quietly – not bother me?" Maggie sighed; a sigh of reluctance tinged with resignation. That was how her life worked; there was no other way forward.

"I will send a card, Sentinel," she told his receding image. "I promised and I will."

※

Sun blazed on the site; blinding; banishing shadow from the landscape. The team worked on in the relentless heat, anxious to accomplish their task; collect relevant samples; ensure that the company had the data needed. They took refuge, in shifts, in the ice-white tents erected for their comfort and shelter from the sun, together with equipment that had to be protected. The tents became stuffy, claustrophobic over time and flies managed to find a way inside. This was the nature of their working environment. But rocks and a chance to see them 'in situ' always drew Maggie to extremes.

Maggie found Mark, her assigned team mate, easy to work alongside. They shared a part of the task; discussed what samples they needed; from where to take them and how to obtain the best results; what to collect and what to reject.

It was two months work that, to Maggie, seemed as if it would go on forever. The heat affected her, this time round. She struggled to keep up. Her energy level flagged. Mark proved supportive; did not realise her predicament as she jammed in the lack of energy; kept it silent within her body. She feigned exuberance, well being and enthusiasm. Mark drew closer. She sensed his need for her; his hope. Maggie ignored the signs; treated him as a friend; a work partner.

※

The final day arrived and the team thankfully packed up; headed back to the town in Jeeps. Maggie anticipated the luxury of two nights in a hotel before the team flew out, leaving dust, heat and the searing sun behind. "Winter. It will be winter." She attempted to imagine winter; an impossibility in around forty degrees.

※

In her room, alone at last, Maggie showered and lay resting in a towelling robe. Sentinel appeared; their time together. She recollected those moments; rewound and played them in her mind until she drifted into light sleep.

❈

A tap at the door. Maggie swung her feet to the floor; called out that she was there.

Mark. Mark was waiting outside.

"Just checking that you're O.K.." He smiled broadly.

"Yes. Yes, I was resting, dozing. It was an exhausting trip."

"And some."

Maggie laughed.

"Fancy a drink?" Mark asked her.

"Mmm. Give me half an hour. I'll meet you in the bar."

"Sure. See you there, Maggie."

She closed the door, raked through her belongings for something to wear. She presumed that they would go on to eat.

Winter. Winter crept into her mind. Maggie hated feeling cold but, somehow, this time around, it stood there inviting her to approach. She shivered; concentrated on dressing for the evening ahead.

❈

Mark waited, leaning against the bar, staring down at his drink. Maggie walked towards him, pleased that he did not pace; look at his watch; as she had been some time in her room. He had allowed her to come to him in her own time.

He realised her approach; smiled and moved to meet her.

"A perfumed beauty!" he exclaimed, and laughed.

"Compliments of the 'bath bottles'," Maggie joked in reply.

"Certainly different from the 'field Maggie' I once knew."

"You haven't scrubbed up badly yourself," she retorted.

Mark pushed a drink along the bar, to her.

"I ordered this for you."

"Thanks."

Maggie took the glass; sipped slowly.

"The others?"

"Have gone out to eat. We can join them. They are just a taxi ride away."

"No thanks, Mark. I'm too tired to socialise. Just want to relax."

"Thought so," he answered. "We can eat here."

Over the meal, Maggie and Mark chatted briefly about the trip; their findings.

"Enough! Enough!" Mark lifted his hands in mock horror.

"You're right. No more 'shop' talk."

They went on to talk about holidays they had taken; holidays they held in mind for the future. Mark had recently been to the U.S. to visit a friend and his wife.

"Been anywhere yourself?"

Maggie hesitated.

"Been too busy," she answered. Sentinel entered her mind.

"Anything planned?"

"Not really. Think I'll chill out at home," she considered. "Sort out a few things. You?"

"No. Same as you. I need to take stock – see what's on the agenda."

After coffee, Maggie leaned towards Mark.

"I'm tired. Think I'll go to bed."

Mark pushed back his chair; stood up.

"Of course. I'll take you up."

"I can find my way, Mark."

He laughed.

"I'll take you, all the same."

In the lift, he held her; gently kissed her forehead. She did not have the heart to push him away. Outside her room, Maggie braced herself for what she supposed was the inevitable.

"Sleep tight. See you at breakfast."

Taken by surprise, "Night Mark. Yes," was all she said.

Mark turned; headed for his own room; or the bar. Key in hand, she closed the door behind her; leaned on it in relief. "No awkward refusal."

Thankful, Maggie undressed; prepared for bed.

The following day, they toured the city as a group. It seemed a fitting farewell. They would eat together that evening; a celebration tinged with commiseration at the dissipation of their team.

※

'Who has seen the wind?'

Christina Rossetti

Chapter Twenty Nine

Spindel

I, Spindel, continue alone. My feet bleed from the pain of parting; rough, unstable shale over which I scrabble for a foothold. My mind grapples with what is akin to a lunar landscape. I am about to be cast adrift; cling to subsist; am afraid of floating free with no wind to carry me.

How long can I hold on; find crevices for my feet before I slide in an agony of despair into the unending void which is space? But my hold is firm; I will it so. A hold taut as stringed instruments reaching for the edges of sound; grating; not well honed nor tuned to the symphony.

I, Spindel, face into the rock to which I cling. It changes before my eyes; becomes transparent. I cling to earth's transparent skin; a voyeur, not a participant. I am excluded. I remain a part of the universe, but am lost; outwith that entity; almost invisible. If I could pierce that skin with a pinprick I, Spindel, could re-enter.

I have no pin.

Now, glass palaces beckon. My mind fills with their image. My hold weakens. I will allow myself to rise there one more time; see Prince Parsu's story as it unfolds in my mind; as it was told to me in another time, another space, by Prince Parsu; who may exist only in my mind and in no other place.

Slowly, I release the grasp I still have, knowing that I have a destination in mind and will no longer float into oblivion. Those stringed instruments begin their melody; more a rhapsody; tuned to perfection; lifting me to where the magnetic pull of the palaces can attract me; draw me in.

※

I, Spindel, return to that time; when I was an embryo mind; aeons before. Prince Parsu sits on a cloud that rests in the vicinity of the city; his city of glass palaces. He sits alone; a small, hunched creature; bejewelled; dressed in rich fabrics; fabrics that may have been woven by the sun's rays. Here, they appear out of place; day invading night. This is how I see him; a droplet of light left behind when the horizon shifted, tilted, on a course that blots out the sun as day turns to night.

The cloud waits as I pass those cold pinnacles of ice; allows me to settle softly in its vapour. Prince Parsu does not see me. I move towards him; sit still by his side. He will not speak to me again to tell his tale; this I know. I must summon his tale to unfold in my mind's eye, as one summons players to perform.

After their meeting in the garden where the small fountain plays, Prince Parsu took Olmi to be his bride, his princess; constructed those palaces of glass that he might see her reflected; myriad, in his vision. She, being young and beautiful, was flattered by the attention of this exotic prince; desired to be all to him as it was in her nature to please; prepared to give him her freedom as a precious gift to hold until it was time to release her. Prince Parsu, being proud, could not countenance at that time the sincerity of her purpose, her actions; nor the value of her precious gift. He knew only that she was to be his and he desired her as a perfect jewel to be added to his vast wealth.

As time drifted, the smile from within faded visibly on Princess Olmi's face. Her skin lost its glow; appeared wan; waxen. Anxious to please his bride; his precious jewel; Prince Parsu filled the city with exotic blooms that scented the air; blazed colour into those walls of glass. Princess Olmi delighted in his eagerness to care for her and gave all she could, in return.

The glow from Princess Olmi's heart once more lit her face, shining through the tiredness she tried to cover. To Prince Parsu, she was no longer a jewel; a desire. Love for Princess Olmi invaded his being as the exotic scents, from the blooms he had imported, claimed the breath of the city, until chill air swept in, drained colour from each bloom; froze each leaf, stem and petal so that they stood, sculpted, against the glass.

Princess Olmi reached out to touch the blooms; shuddered and trembled as she felt the icy substance. Unable to coax life into their sheer rigidity, she backed away, her fingers cut and bleeding; that red the only colour within the glass walls containing her.

Prince Parsu returned that night. Pools of water glinted in the starlight. The blooms had melted as the wind had receded. He found Princess Olmi lying on her low bed of down, which warmed her chilled body; but, the ice had claimed her soul. Princess Olmi stared at Prince Parsu; no expression in that gaze.

"Olmi." Prince Parsu was on his knees beside her, beseeching her to return to him; to no avail.

As night surrounded the palace with the depth of its fathomless velvet, Prince Parsu remained at Olmi's side.

"What have I done?" he chided himself and wished time backwards; to the day they first met. Time could not be bought, although he would give all he owned for it to be so.

※

Prince Parsu could not rest, the image of Olmi before him; always. He craved more of her; constructed palace after palace, each of glass. There, he placed her image, to walk freely; his one image of Olmi reflected in each wall so that she filled the city with her presence; visible to him alone.

"That is why," he told me, "I return to sit here to be consumed by Olmi, my princess, my bride."

These were the last words I heard him speak.

Why had he appeared to me? Why do I, Spindel, keep returning to the city of glass palaces? To remind myself of his fate; a fate I have no desire to duplicate. And Segment will return to her own. I cannot possess her, capture all that she is, nor make her mine. Segment is a guide that I follow willingly. She will guide me to the path I know that I must follow, until ...

but I, Spindel, refuse to contemplate a time, a place.

Chapter Thirty

Maggie

Maggie let herself in. The flat was cold. She shivered; opened the door to her bedroom and dumped her luggage there. She wandered through to the kitchen, feeling disorientated after the long flight and by the dramatic drop in temperature. She filled the kettle. Something hot to drink; something she could warm her hands on. She needed to think.

Drink in hand, Maggie realised that she had not turned on the heating. "Why would I? I haven't needed heat for some time." Standing the mug on the table she crossed the room, to the switch.

She sat on the sofa turning a postcard over and over in her hands, then, put it on the coffee table and picked up her drink; immediate comfort. She contemplated the postcard where it lay; on the upper side, a busy foreign city; on the underside blank space apart from the small print. She had taken it from her hand luggage, a small bag which lay beside her, when she sat down. She recalled her last night in that city; the almost false gaiety covering the team's inner desire to be away from that place; back home.

✺

After the meal, when they all arrived back at the hotel and had uttered final 'goodbyes', she and Mark took the elevator to the roof terrace; sat contemplating the stars; the city's skyline. There was a slight breeze, warm, caressing. Mark put his arm round her shoulders.

"Romantic."

Maggie laughed.

"If you say so."

"There is a certain glamour to it," he insisted.

"The city or the sky?"

"The city – from up here."

"But we know how it really is – down there."

"True."

"The sky, though," Maggie began, "is different – a vast, largely unknown, universe."

"One could lose oneself, that's for sure."

"Exactly," agreed Maggie.

Mark had given her a curious look. Maggie had shrugged.

"We need sleep," she said.

Mark stood up; unnecessarily helped her to her feet. They stepped back inside.

Outside the door to her room, Mark had hesitated.

"Come in," she had said, sensing that closure was needed.

"You sure?"

"Are you?" Maggie turned the question back on him.

"I get the feeling that you are trying to complete something that has not had a chance to begin." Mark had surprised her in saying this.

"I would rather see you again. You intrigue me, Maggie."

She had laughed; kissed his nose.

"Very astute. Safe flight back."

Mark had hugged her, grinned, and set off along the corridor.

※

She recalled the relief she had felt and considered that she should not, perhaps, have placed herself on offer. It also pleased her that Mark had, in a way, called her bluff. Maggie knew that they would meet again officially, to complete the project at this end; knew that Mark would treat her well; felt terror at that thought of 'belonging'; pushed it away and turned over the postcard.

"What would I write?" she asked herself, knowing that she had promised Sentinel a contact number or address; information only; not email – too instant and visible. Why was she contemplating more? He stood before her eyes, in her mind. She settled on a mobile number.

"It cannot. We cannot," she told his apparition, but a longing welled, somewhere in her inner being.

Maggie suddenly hated the flat; being back.

"Tomorrow," she announced to the walls, "tomorrow, I shall drive to the bungalow – take the postcard."

This, she reasoned on reflection, would be because she had no actual address for Sentinel. She had not written it down, or maybe had and had not kept it. Of course, the card would reach him by post as there were few houses in that area. But in delivering it by hand, Sentinel was certain to receive it. And, if he were to be out, it would surprise him on his return.

※

Maggie, true to her own word, set off early the following morning. It was cold. But the sky looked bright.

As she neared her destination, after several hours of driving, Maggie smiled in anticipation of seeing the bungalow again.

Why had she left so suddenly? It was her way of staving off commitment. She envisaged this visit as a brief exchange of pleasantries, although she knew this to be almost an impossibility. Would Sentinel be hurt - resentful? She hoped not.

Maggie felt exhaustion almost overwhelm her and pulled in, onto the grass verge. Soon, the sea would be in sight. Now, she needed to rest; gather courage to continue. Or, she could turn back, leave the postcard at a local post office.

Half an hour later, Maggie roused herself, stepped out of the car and breathed deeply. The purity of the air, filled with a tang from the sea, energised her. She determined to go on.

Maggie could see the bungalow and drove slowly towards it. She hoped that Sentinel would be as he had been when they were together, here.

"Just so that I don't have to make an effort."

Friends. That is how she restructured it in her mind; close friends.

There was a sign standing in the grass at one side of the drive. Maggie frowned; the sign so unexpected that she was shocked.

FOR SALE

it read and superimposed,

SOLD

"Is Sentinel still here?" Maybe a silly question to ask herself. Hoping against hope, she climbed from the driving seat and set off on foot, up the drive; not taking the car to the door. It was obvious that the bungalow stood empty. The curtains were pulled together. Her knock sounded hollow. Maggie forced the postcard through the stiff letterbox, turned and ran to the car.

Inside, she sobbed, bent over the steering wheel; experienced total emptiness within. Remembering that she had parked at the end of the drive and that the new owners might return, Maggie reached for a tissue; blotted her tears; blew her nose; revved the engine.

The hours back seemed endless; the sky had darkened, moving towards evening.

"Perhaps. Perhaps, Sentinel will find the postcard. Perhaps, the new owners will forward it to the original owner and he will give it to Sentinel."

The opportunity had been lost. She pushed it in with every other missed or lost opportunity. Shut them out; locked them away.

"But I never throw away the key," she mocked herself.

※

The flat felt cold, having had little chance to build up warmth. She saw that Mark had left a message on the answer phone.

"Tomorrow. I'll listen to it tomorrow."

Maggie drank a glass of water and crawled under the duvet. She had not eaten all day.

"Fool," she told herself." Tomorrow," she whispered and fell, exhausted, into sleep.

'A particle is a small localized object with mass and charge, and it is only in one position in space at an instant'

Shan Gao

Chapter Thirty One

Spindel

I, Spindel, allow myself to float; away from Prince Parsu, his present and his past. In so doing, I detach from my own past. Pain sears my mind; to remain in the past, the pain of my past, draws me. I will not indulge. In my mind, I sever the string; that of a lute or lyre. A beautiful pain which pierces heart and soul. I sense that I am lost; rootless. All around is black; deep black. I could suffocate in its blanket; easily. But Segment, a particle of hope, floats as a mote across an eye. I cannot go where it seems that none has trod before; give leeway to that which desires to grasp and engulf me. I, Spindel, must find the thread that leads to Segment. As she has hoped for me, I clutch at hope. This space I thought to claim is not my own; a false cavity.

I do not allow black its hold on me; force through that dread heaviness. I chanced upon that particle signifying hope. It cannot be still. It moves. If I follow, it will become a glimmer; this I know. Eventually, Segment will be with me.

I wake with a jolt; as if I have fallen from a height. Have I fallen from that rock to which I clung in that time before I met with Prince Parsu one last time? Was that time only moments ago or deep in time's past? I cannot tell. Shivering, I raise myself from the ground; that rough shale which offers no comfort; no pity.

Segment waits in the future it seems. She is a part of the final movement to be born when conditions dictate, become united in one moment; one time in that instant, perfect, only for its creation. Those intricate, closing bars play now, in my mind. Jarring within my brain motions the need to discard what is unnecessary; false notes, discord, phrases which belong elsewhere.

I, Spindel, wrap myself in my thoughts and stand; prepare to carry myself forward to the conclusion. My destiny lies ahead, not behind. Those moments in time, in space, are not where I am. I am in this time, this space, until I arrive in another. It seems that I cajole myself with riddles; conundrums. Is this self deception?

I am Spindel; alone at this time; alone with thoughts that are mine alone. I am outwith, but must strive to enter. Why? I must taste the fruit that lies within; touch the experience to find what I am not.

I ache with thoughts, but remain wrapped in them. I shall carry them the distance; lay them before Segment. Leave them? That moment will arrive.

The shale is less jagged. I have found a smoother path.

Chapter Thirty Two

Sentinel

That morning, Sentinel took possession of the keys for the bungalow after putting a final signature to paper. Now, he had a refuge; a home.

Drinking coffee, he contemplated; all that he owned he had packed into the second hand car which he had bought and he was about to leave; possibly there would be work available in the area where he was to live, in the near future. He smiled; felt as a child beginning an adventure; excitement welled combined with a sense of freedom. He glanced about him at fellow coffee drinkers. "Were they, too, embarking on an adventure – taking a different path?" he mused. "Perhaps not."

Sentinel recaptured the day when he and Maggie shared coffee; wished that she was with him and that they could share this adventure; this future. He had not heard from her. He had realised some time ago that she had no specific point of contact; but she had found him before. Regret crawled towards him. "How could 'today' have ended so abruptly? How could tomorrow ever arrive?" Yet it had. This 'today' was tomorrow; a new beginning; the past a completed section.

He stared into his cup at the dregs of his coffee; deflated. How could he face 'tomorrow' without Maggie? The thought weighed on him. Sentinel glanced to the right of his cup. The keys, his keys, lay there; the keys for the car and for his first home. Taking them up, he resolved to continue his adventure; to embrace the hardship and the joy. As a child, he had clambered over obstacles placed before him; or had found a way around them. Sentinel pushed away the chair, walked to the till, paid and left.

The car awaited him. He crossed the road, opened the door, climbed in and prepared to leave. Feelings for Maggie and the loss of her presence, filled him again. Sentinel sensed that his hope for 'tomorrow' would drive him on. Today, he had Alice to thank for her generosity; for her understanding. He had a photograph of her that Mr. Greyling had kindly given him. "Had Alice left her photographs to her solicitor?" he wondered. He turned the key in the ignition to start the car engine and pulled away from the kerb.

Sentinel desired both to arrive and to be forever travelling towards his haven; his refuge; this a journey of mixed emotions. He moved towards the new experience; hoped unrealistically; to discover that Maggie was not there waiting, an unbearable image at the back of his mind. He recited poetry; took in each aspect of the journey as though it was his first visit. Later, a favourite album accompanied his thoughts; lines spoke to him as he listened:

'Oh, the day it will come when my travelling is done
And I'll search for a light on the shoreline ……'

Would Maggie search his shoreline?

※

At last; the road out to the bungalow! 'Home'. Sentinel laughed; it was. He imagined it spelled out in pebbles on the field grass; burned into wood on a rustic sign at the edge of the drive; daubed in paint across the brickwork. But it would remain imprinted, secretly, within his being.

The bungalow stood solitary in its surroundings; neither attractive nor ugly; more functional; a roof over his head. Suddenly, he could not wait to be inside; to draw, to write; to be himself entirely; stood at the brink of his new life.

Sentinel drove slowly up the drive, stepped from the car and walked to the door; his door. He unlocked the door, pushed and stepped inside. The door scraped over paper; card. A postcard lay there, on the floor. He bent to pull it from beneath the door; picked it up and turned it over. The postcard pictured some hot city. It was probably for the previous owner. He turned it back. There he saw it; a mobile number and a small 'm' at the bottom; as if shyly added. Sentinel felt weak; grasped the postcard to him and walked to the couch where he sat down, gazing at the cryptic signature.

"There is no address," it dawned on him. "Maggie did not post this. She delivered it. Maggie has been here. When? How long ago? Is she here, now?" Sentinel jumped up; ran to the door; looked out. Only the car stood there. "What if?" Sentinel resolved to look for 'B&Bs', guest houses, hotels in the area. He would check each one. He ran to the car. The door to the bungalow stood open. He ran back, turned the key, still in the lock, and set off.

After two hours of frantic searching, fruitless enquiries, he became aware that evening darkness approached. He needed to eat, to return to sort out belongings; and thoughts.

※

The following day, Sentinel woke with new hope for 'tomorrow'. He would not give up; must contact Maggie; tell her that he was here; explain his situation; that the bungalow was now his home. With this in mind, he looked round.

The bungalow was as he had left it. The contents were included in the purchase price. He stood in the doorway to Maggie's room remembering her presence. His own belongings, stacked and piled just inside the door, he would unpack today.

Maggie? Sentinel considered whether or not he should ring the number on the postcard. He had agreed that he would not seek her out. But, she had no contact for him. The sign outside told that the bungalow had been sold. She would not expect to find him here. She had found him before, but that contact was no longer available as his former colleague had moved on; lived and worked elsewhere. He decided that he should ring the number just to tell Maggie that he was here.

Later. To ring now would interrupt his feelings of expectancy. He would look forward to 'later'. Sentinel knew that he feared rejection, but reasoned that Maggie would probably be working and not in a position to talk. And what would he say? "Maggie, the bungalow is mine. That's where I am – live." Something like that. He would rehearse as he unpacked.

※

It was done. His home had been created, much as his garden refuge had been, all those years before. Sentinel sat drinking tea, waiting for reality to take hold. "Now. Now is the time to ring," he told himself. The card lay on the coffee table in front of him with the number side uppermost. Tentatively, he dialled Maggie's number.

It rang out.

The Moorings

'From the dark salty sea I found refuge in thee
But I'm soon to be loosening my moorings'

Andrew Duhon

Chapter Thirty Three

Spindel

The way is easier, now. I, Spindel, know the direction in which my destiny lies; cross the bar lines. Notes rise and fall in constant creation. The previous movement, slow in ascendency, soars to its apex; falls to make way for the melody which follows.

The shale pathway narrows; becomes firm as earth holds fast its stones. I step freely; face the breeze that caresses my face, smooth and harmonious in both sound and touch. I hear tinkling bells across the breeze; their source a spring ahead that passes beneath the path. I rest at its side; quench my thirst as the combination of sounds quenches my soul; that concept of soul which is within my mind but outwith the realm of Spindel. It is Sentinel I, Spindel, seek to refresh. He draws ever nearer. We cannot separate for ever. I stop. Segment. I draw thoughts of Segment to be uppermost; force Sentinel to a lower, more distant, place.

※

I, Spindel, march on; the pace exhilarating. Segment is ahead, where our paths rejoin; our melodies merge. But, I cannot contemplate this fully as it lies ahead.

The turf springs beneath my feet; for that is what it has become; no shale; no stones. I progress light of foot, as the way inclines, placing strength in my direction. I, Spindel, do not falter, nor do my feet miss a beat. All that I have stored is waiting to emerge; the symphony near to completion. I have brought it this far in crude form, but it will be performed perfectly; that time will come.

My pace slows as the inclination becomes more steep. I shall reach the summit; see clearly what lies ahead. Before I push forward to the brink; at which point I must consider as, beyond it, there is no turning back; I, Spindel, sit on the turf beneath a clear sky; breathe fragrance of grass peppered, now, I see with daisies; small, delicate, with nesting golden orbs that tilt to the sun. A new motif enters the score to reflect this vision. The notes are quick, clear; joyous.

Segment, my muse, hovers before me as I envisage her. Her form is no longer as solid; or, I cannot recall that solidity. She appears semi translucent; shimmers; perhaps she always did.

To dawdle is folly. I rise. The moment is closer than I had supposed. I must not miss the moment; forfeit all.

※

I, Spindel, stand at the brink. Before me lies the final movement. What I see brings terror. I am cold; covered in sea fret shaken off by waves that tower, crash; churn in a chasm below. This movement bursts with overwhelming sound;

behind it devastating silence; signifying the beginning of the end piece.

Disorientation attempts to whirl me; force my feet from this spot where I employ total willpower to remain firmly planted. I do not want to experience the future; fill with fear.

Chapter Thirty Four

Maggie

Maggie set off for the meeting; more a collaboration with the client, following the field trip. Mark had left a message suggesting that they go on from the meeting and share a meal, or something. She had agreed. Her notes and laptop, holding statistics and test results, lay on the passenger seat. Not far to go; that was a relief. She still felt tired from the trip.

※

She and Mark stepped out into the sunshine. Everything had gone well, the client satisfied that they had all done a good job ; had confidence, now, knowing that the site was ideal for their project. Thanks and handshakes terminated the meeting; brought closure as far as Maggie and Mark were concerned. They had passed on their data; stood in the street outside, free to move on.

"Well? What do you think, Maggie? Are you hungry?"

"Perhaps a walk, Mark. It's good to be in the fresh air."

"There's a park just round the corner," volunteered Mark. "Would that suit?"

"Yes. Sounds good."

They set off. Mark was right. The park appeared as an oasis, set within the busy streets.

"I imagine it fills up with office workers in the summer, at lunch time," said Maggie.

The wrought iron gates stood open; inviting entry. Maggie pulled up her collar; the sun at this time of year not strong enough to ease the chill in the air.

"It's really not strolling weather, Maggie. More a brisk walk." Maggie nodded agreement.

"And then we can consider where to eat," continued Mark.

To begin with, they walked in silence. There did not seem much common ground. They had left behind their time together as the meeting concluded. "What now?" Maggie asked herself.

Mark spoke.

"Strange, now that things have come to an end," he said, "we can't really think of what to say. We need to begin again. A first date," he laughed.

Maggie glanced at him. He could be so old fashioned.

"What are you saying, Mark?"

He shrugged.

"Just that I like you, Maggie. I wouldn't want us to walk away. Not yet."

"Right." What did *she* want? She had no idea, but she felt hungry; needed to eat.

"Let's eat, Mark. Do you know somewhere?"

Maggie knew that he had stayed overnight as he lived further away; too far to drive that morning.

"Not really, but I'm sure we'll find something. If not, there's the hotel. It's just round the next corner. That's how I knew about the park."

"I sort of guessed that," said Maggie. "Shall we go there, then?"

"Suits me," answered Mark and they left the park.

※

The service had been slow at the hotel, although not many people were eating. There was opportunity for conversation, but not much was said that held any significance. They had shared stories and talked about geology in general.

"Maggie. Why don't we have coffee in my room? I haven't checked out, yet, and it's less formal than here. We need to thaw out."

Maggie laughed and stood up.

"Come on then."

They made their way to the lifts.

On the fourth floor, Mark opened the door to his room. They went inside. Mark turned her round; held her by the shoulders.

"Where are we going?" he asked.

"Well we're here, aren't we?" Maggie retorted and leaned in towards him.

"You sure?" Mark asked as she broke away.

"Sure."

As they moved towards the bed. Maggie kicked off her shoes; threw her jacket onto a chair. Mark unbuttoned her top and she his shirt. They abandoned their tops. Maggie threw herself back onto the bed. Mark lay down beside her.

"Maggie."

"Go ahead."

Mark sat up.

"What do you mean, Maggie, 'go ahead'?"

Maggie stared up at him.

"Just that. Go ahead. It's what you want – what you've wanted for a long while."

Stunned, Mark considered her words.

"O.K. Maggie, yes it is. But not in this way. Don't you see that I care for you. To me, you are someone special. Someone I had hoped to meet."

She looked away.

"Don't look away, Maggie! What do *you* want?"

What did she want? She had no idea. She had known that it would come to this when she had listened to his message. She felt drawn to Mark. He was an honourable person; someone you could trust. Why was she behaving in this way? She turned to him.

"I'm sorry, Mark."

Tears welled. Mark leaned over and kissed her.

"Don't worry. Shall we start again?"

He caressed her as he spoke. Maggie was aroused; responded.

"I do care, Maggie."

He was tender, thoughtful and passionate in such a caring manner. Maggie could hardly bear it, but craved him all the same.

When it was over, he lay beside her.

"Thank you," he said.

"My pleasure," she smiled.

Mark fondled her hair.

"It's not a physical 'thank you', Maggie. It's a 'thank you' for sharing – for giving us a beginning."

Maggie had no words to say.

After a while, he sat up.

"I have to go, Maggie."

She sat up; began to dress.

"It was lovely, Mark," she offered.

"Yes," he agreed.

They dressed in silence.

"Maggie."

"Yes."

"I need to see you again. I want to get to know you. You intrigue me."

"I intrigue myself," she thought, but smiled at Mark.

"Can I? Can we?" he asked.

Maggie stood ready to leave.

"What do you want of me, Mark?"

"I had hoped – we could be together – have a relationship." he answered.

She felt cold; about to shiver. She looked back at Mark, directly; laid down her jacket and moved over to him. She knew that he was genuine; that he would care for her and treat her well. He was a safe haven, yet her whole being pushed him away and she could not understand why.

"Mark. You are a wonderful person – kind, caring, fun to be with on field trips. If I could, I would say, 'yes we can', but I can't, Mark. I just can't. Mark, I don't even know why I can't. There is someone out there, Mark – someone for you – but I am not that person. I would destroy you, Mark, as I destroy myself."

Mark held her tightly.

"Maggie. Maggie, it doesn't have to be this way. I can help you."

"No, Mark. No, you can't. You don't understand."

Maggie pulled away; picked up her jacket and bag. She took his hand in hers.

"Mark, you are so sweet. Thank you. I needed you this afternoon. Had planned it, even."

She let go of his hand and moved to the door. Before she stepped out into the corridor, she turned back.

"Thank you," she whispered.

And left.

Chapter Thirty Five

Sentinel

Sentinel had not tried Maggie's number for several days. The rebuff of its ringing out shook his confidence. He spent the days finding places for his belongings; not that there were many; shopped for food, and for a small frame in which to keep safe the photograph of Alice. It stood above the fireplace. He looked on it with fondness and gratitude that she had afforded him this home. He wondered why Maggie had not picked up his call; returned it.

It was cold and bright. Sentinel took a scarf and gloves; decided to walk. He walked round the field, a plot in actuality, but the thought of its being a field felt more satisfying. He looked over at sheep in the field behind and at the bungalow from different angles. He had almost made it his, in his mind, but not quite. Still, it seemed strange; dreamlike. He walked down the drive and along the road, away from the village.

His thoughts were of Maggie. This should be her home, too. It was incomplete without her. Would she return? Was it a possibility? Perhaps. Perhaps not. He pushed forward, striding out. An old man was headed towards him.

"New here?" he called out.

Surprised, Sentinel hesitated.

"Yes. Yes, I live back there."

He indicated behind him.

"Then, you're the fellow who's bought the bungalow."

"Yes."

The man grinned, satisfied that he had everything in its place. He raised a hand in a farewell gesture as he walked on. Sentinel acknowledged it.

After an hour, he turned back. The sun was rapidly losing the small amount of heat that it had radiated earlier. There would be a spectacular sunset.

Arriving home; yes, it was home; he wandered once more around the property. Meeting the old man and the walk had finally instilled in him a sense of belonging. He had a home; a home that would not be snatched from him; destroyed. Warmth filled his being and he made his way back inside, to the kitchen to prepare a meal.

In the evening, he looked through paperwork. "I must sort and file this," he thought. "Tomorrow, I'll head into the town and buy files. There should be a stationers." He refilled his glass with wine; sat back and relaxed. He closed his eyes and Maggie appeared. "Where are you?" he wondered. "Can I bring you back here? Would you come?" It was easy to ask an apparition; a figment of the imagination. Sentinel remained with his eyes closed and watched memory unfold the time that they had spent here. It was an ecstatic form of torture that the memory showed up so clearly. He could hear her voice. He felt bewitched; overpowered by her presence.

Suddenly, the door to memory closed and she was gone. He knew that tears ran down his face. Maggie. He sobbed for Maggie, burying his head in a cushion in an attempt to ease the anguish. It seemed that his heart would rend.

Sentinel woke. It was cold and dark. He felt stiff; in need of bed and sleep. He made his way to the bedroom; to claim oblivion for the night.

✵

As each day passed, Sentinel experienced mixed emotion. He knew that, without Maggie, he was incomplete. He needed to summon courage to try her number once more. Two days before, he had managed to do this. Again, it rang out. Why? He could not understand why she had given him the number only to leave his calls unanswered.

Sentinel felt himself at the edge of a precipice; before him stretched the unknown. He could turn back, build a new life here, alone, or he could step out to join Maggie; if he could find her; if she would have him. He picked up the phone; dialled Maggie's number. It rang; kept on ringing.

"Hello."

A faint voice responded.

"Maggie?"

His heart thumped.

"Yes."

"Maggie, it's Sentinel."

"Sentinel?"

"You remember."

"Yes, I remember."

"You left me this number."

"You went back to the bungalow?"

There was an element of surprise in Maggie's voice.

"Yes. It's mine, Maggie."

"Yours?"

"I bought it."

"Bought it?"

"Yes. It's my home."

"You're living there?"

"Yes."

"Oh."

Sentinel could not place the tone of her last utterance.

"Maggie. Where are you?"

"I can't tell you."

Her tone had changed.

"Maggie? Maggie, I'm not coming to hunt you down."

"No."

"No. I just wanted to say that I am here – because you had no means of knowing that."

"No. I suppose not."

"You can visit – if you want to."

"I can't"

"Oh."

Sentinel heard the disappointment in his voice.

"Are you busy working?"

"No."

"I wondered – wondered why you are not really talking."

"I'm tired. I have been away working. I'm back now."

"Is that why you did not pick up on my calls?"

"No. No, I had left the phone at a hotel. It was sent to someone who had been staying there. He sent it on to me."

"Ah. It's good to hear you, Maggie."

"You, too."

"Maggie. Could you give me an address? I promise not to come looking. It's just that if you lose the phone, I have nothing."

"Does that matter?"

"Of course."

"Well, yes. Wait a moment …"

Sentinel sat with his ear to the phone, waiting for her return. He heard her reading out an address; quickly grabbed a pencil; scribbled it on the back of an envelope lying on the coffee table.

"Satisfied?"

What was that? Sentinel heard the change in her tone. Who was she punishing?

"Maggie."

"I have to go."

"Wait a minute. Please. Maggie, don't punish yourself. I won't hurt you."

"Got to go."

"Maggie. Remember that."

The phone went dead.

Sentinel fell back, exhausted. Maggie. He had spoken to Maggie; had heard her voice; a voice that wrenched the roots of his being. Maggie, he knew, was tearing herself apart and to know that tore at his own fabric. He experienced searing pain. What could he do? Maggie had opened up, encouraged him to be the person she knew he could be. Alice. She, too, had 'freed' him from his childhood.

Maggie still buried herself in her past; would not or could not let it go. He would phone again; in a few days; just chat casually, hoping that she would feel his warmth; his concern. He clutched at the envelope. He had an address. This made him feel safer; as if he held a lifeline.

Maggie. Maggie, his centre; his nucleus.

'Niños Del Cielo'

'Todo lo que perdemos suma una cifra
unica, la nuestra. Si perdieras algo tuyo
algo que no estaba destinado a perderse,
tu cifra seria inexacta para siempre'

Claudia Masin

'All that we lose is summed up in a unique
code, ours. If you were to lose something of yours
that was not destined to be lost,
your code would be inexact forever'

translation Ann Sharples

Chapter Thirty Six

Spindel

When I, Spindel, first encountered Segment; for that is what she is, one of many that move as one entity; I saw her qualities. She is a segment of truth; not the whole truth but a segment of truth that can be realised.

When I, Spindel, first encountered Segment, her note soared. I felt the sound of her. It drew me as panpipes enticing a nymph. Was I the piper? But, it was the truth that drew us for its own purpose; the truth that we existed in that time, that space; in that instant of meeting.

※

I, Spindel, blink it clear and stare ahead. The way has changed; the sea frozen, captured in motion and held motionless. Waves tower as a sculpted forest curved against a gale. Below, in each pit, an ice path leads to the foot of that opposite cliff; to where I must make my way. Shards of ice project, pinned to the cliff where my descent awaits me. I, Spindel, will bear the agony of that descent to re-encounter Sentinel until we rise to the pinnacle of sound in which the symphony is contained.

I experience cold; ice cold; cold that suspends my being for an instant before I fill with extraordinary warmth; the warmth of wonder. Segment is at my side. She wraps a fur about me and holds it still. I fumble to close it against the cold; confused. Is this an hallucination; the trickery of a dream?

"Spindel."

She speaks. I reach out to touch her. She is real.

"Spindle, I will accompany you to the close of your journey. We shall travel together. Close your eyes, Spindel."

I close the eyes of my mind and float. I know that Segment is there; have no fear that I may lose her because she is outwith my sight. I am light; a feather, perhaps. My feet walk; transport me. I feel soft grass as I tread.

"Open your eyes, Spindel!" Segment directs.

And I see that we are at the edge of a meadow. A stream runs beside it; clear and fresh. I, Spindel, lower myself to the ground; taste the spring water; quench my thirst. Segment watches. She shimmers in the sunlight; as strong and as fragile as a dragonfly wing. I stand.

"It is almost time, Spindel. I am but a speck of dust hovering in the air. I am a particle in your imagination; a figment awaiting its release. Your symphony is almost composed. I, Segment, am your muse; the essence. As you release me to go to my own, the way to that specific time, that exact place, will open."

All that is within me desires to claim Segment, but I cannot follow the path of Prince Parsu. I must allow her to go.

"Spindel. Release me, now. Return to Sentinel where *your* time and place wait."

I, Spindel, hesitate.

"Do it," her soft voice urges and I can see that she cannot bear to stay longer.

I, Spindel, close my mind to her so that she can return to her own. I sink to the ground in an agony of anguish and despair. Remain there. Time passes. I am aware of a presence; look up. Sentinel stands there. He waits. I had not noticed him before. He is where I parted from him; in that time, that place. I see that it is my time also; my place. I have erred, wandered; sought another existence, alone.

Obedient now, I stand and move towards him. Together, we can be a single persona; each balances the other; a harmony that will echo in the future. Does he know that I approach? He appears not to see me.

I permit the form I took upon myself to become invisible; dissipate; no longer a valid entity. I forgo that existence; relinquish the music that I have composed to allow Sentinel to become complete; one.

I, as Spindel the composer, perform my final act.

Chapter Thirty Seven

Maggie

It had not been quite as Maggie had let Sentinel suppose; the situation with her phone. Yes, it had fallen out of her bag in the hotel room and she had not realised. The hotel had contacted Mark; sent it on to him. In turn, Mark had sent it on to Maggie. But, the chain had not taken long to complete. Maggie had seen Sentinel's first call; ignored it. When the second call came, she allowed it to ring out; sat frozen, unable to consider what to say.

Why had she done this? She did not know. Perhaps she wanted no past; no future; only present. That way, life was easier to control. So she had thought.

Her tiredness persisted. A colleague firmly advised her,

"Check it out, Maggie. You could be carrying something from your last trip."

Reluctantly, she made an appointment, hoping to appease the woman; divert attention from herself. Maggie felt irritated by the whole situation; it imposed on her independence.

Now, she had to wait for results; was afraid; stupidly so, she thought, and attempted to erase it from her mind. She may not even go for the results. Whatever it was would surely work its way out of her system; eventually.

Maggie sat on a bench outside the hospital; gazed at the stark image of trees etched against the bright winter sky. No breeze; a gentle stillness; a breath held. No thought came to her of the consequences of the results. A white mist obscured the content of her mind.

"I cannot think," her initial thought. "I don't want to think," the second.

Suddenly, her past crowded her mind. The parent who was not her mother stood there. The image of her two dimensional mother in her happiness, captured on film, gazed from her printed position at that of her father; the promise of their future, as a family, shattered before it began.

She could not see herself, but felt the essence of her childhood; as bereft as those leafless trees. Somewhere, a harsh voice of authority pronounced her a thief. Sentinel appeared. The clarity of truth rang clearly in her mind. No. She had not been a thief; then. She had become a thief of her own choosing and in so doing had stolen time. Yes. She was a thief. She had stolen the time that she and Sentinel could have spent together. Maggie could find no reason as to why she had done so. And now, a thief was taking her time.

Maggie shivered. Cold had worked its way through her coat. She felt tired, yet fired with a strange energy. What time she could conserve she could give to Sentinel; in recompense for that which she had stolen.

Nothing appeared real; not at this moment; her life an

uncharted journey. Sentinel waited; she knew; for their future to begin.

※

The following day, Maggie spent going through her belongings; what to keep and what to consign to the growing pile that she intended to discard. There was not that much. She was not a hoarder. Pebbles and rock samples were her treasure. She would keep a handful; especially the 'story pebble'. Books. Notes and writing. These, being mostly functional and connected to work and study, could go. She stored thoughts and not words. Clothes; mostly casual, but the occasional glaring outfit left over from functions intermittently attended. And a couple of smart suits for meetings. They could go to charity.

Maggie threw them in a pile and lay down on the bed; stared at the ceiling as if it was a blank canvas. She threw images onto it, from her past; her mind recoiled; closed down the projector. She scribbled words and phrases in their place, then blinked and they were discarded.

Sentinel. She wrote 'Sentinel' and gazed upon the word in her mind; its contents projected, now, on the ceiling, just to the right of a small plaster crack. When would she tell him? No. The answer was 'no', she would not.

"I could just call – say 'hi'," she thought. And closed her eyes.; too tired to think further.

※

Several more days passed. Maggie had not contacted Sentinel.

"I'm still a thief," she mused as she buttered toast for her breakfast. "Perhaps that is what I want to be."

Later in the day, she sat on the edge of the sofa and dialled Sentinel's number, guilty that she had put off the call she intended to make. There was no answer.

"Maybe he's out walking and left his phone behind. I would do that – if I was out walking."

Maggie envisaged the landscape; desired to be there; out walking.

"Could I drive?" she asked herself. "Too tired," the answer.

※

One day, Maggie cursed as she woke; cursed the pain invading her body. She had a prescription for this; when it was needed; had pushed it to the back of a drawer, denying its existence. Now; this very minute; she needed it. She waited patiently, calmly, allowing the pain to subside, before dressing to walk down to the chemist's.

Waiting in the queue, she held onto the pain that once more, began to take hold. Her turn came. Thankfully, Maggie received the drug she needed and returned to the flat.

Tears streamed down her cheeks as she waited for relief to come. Afterwards, sank back in exhaustion onto the cushion behind her head; and slept.

The room was chilled when she roused herself; light fading. Maggie reached for a lamp switch; clicked it on.

"Tomorrow," she thought, "tomorrow I shall phone Sentinel; see how he is."

※

Two days later, as sunlight filled the room, Maggie picked up the phone; dialled Sentinel's number.

"Hi," she said as he answered her call.

"Maggie!" Sentinel exclaimed at the end of the line.

"Yes, it's me, Sentinel." Maggie experienced a surge of joy as she spoke his name; heard his voice responding to hers. "Where have you been?"

"Nowhere, really, Maggie. Although I went walking for a couple of days."

"Thought so," she almost whispered into the phone.

" I bought a tent," he continued, not hearing her, "thought I'd try it out."

"Isn't it a bit cold for that, Sentinel?"

Again, she felt compelled to speak out his name. She heard him laugh.

"Yes, it was. But the tent was quite cosy, considering that it rained, too – so, it's been well tested."

Maggie laughed this time.

"You didn't get my call?"

"Oh, Maggie! Sorry. I sort of forgot about the phone. I didn't take it with me. No one important calls, really, so I forgot to check when I came home."

"Home. He said 'home'."

"It doesn't matter," she replied.

"Sorry, though. I would have liked to talk earlier than this."

Maggie winced. The pain was returning; the effect of the medication wearing off.

"Maggie?"

"Yes." She forced an upbeat tone to reply.

"You O.K.?"

"Why?"

"Keep the answers short, Maggie," she told herself.

"You sounded a bit odd."

"No."

The pain escalated. She gasped, tried not to groan.

"Maggie. Maggie, you're not all right. I can hear you. Are you in pain?"

"A little," she heard herself admit in a whisper.

"I'm coming to see you," she heard him say.

"Sentinel."

He had hung up.

Maggie crawled to the bedroom, where the medication lay on the bedside table; sat in agony on the bed; swallowed the dose and curled as a foetus, willing the pain gone.

※

Later, she woke and moved under the covers. But the pain was still there, gnawing; a dull ache in the background. Again, it was returning in strength and yet – and yet, could she take more medication? Maggie fumbled in the drawer for the number she had been given, slid her phone from her pocket, where it had stayed since the call to Sentinel; dialled the number; gasped her query; cut off the call to deal with the escalation of pain.

"Why? Why? I want to be left alone," she called out to the walls. They were sending someone round; to assess how she was coping. Horror gripped Maggie. She wanted no one; wanted desperately to be alone; alone with this gross pain. She could become used to it.

※

The doorbell rang. Maggie had nursed her pain as best she could; as if it was an infant in need of nurture. She forced herself upright and moved through to the hallway and the door; released the lock.

※

When she woke, Maggie was uncertain of where she lay. A voice spoke.

"Maggie, we brought you here. You collapsed as you let us in. It will be better for you. We told a neighbour where you are, in case anyone is looking for you. Is there someone we can call?"

Maggie digested the information and smiled.

"No. Thank you."

She floated peacefully; free of responsibility; free of the body that was deserting her.

Chapter Thirty Eight

Sentinel

As he lay in his tent, Sentinel experienced a coming together; a completion. He had made the decision to leave the bungalow for a few days to consider, before phoning Maggie. His phone lay on the kitchen table. He needed time and space to think.

Although it was cold, being winter, Sentinel had not been deterred. He felt that he stood on the edge of a precipice; about to fall. He fought his mind; willed himself to remain upright, to be able to step back; away from time itself.

He had slept fitfully; dreamed vividly at night. Struggled, his tent on his back, into harsh elements; unrelenting weather; during the day.

And now, in mid afternoon, as he lay exhausted; spent; it happened; this transformation. His mind reunited with itself, although he had not known that it had split entirely. Strange melodies, in harmony, played within his mind behind the pattern of his life. That which had passed and that which was to come, fused. A complete life; from beginning to end; a symphony. He could walk forwards with confidence; himself the composer or the symphony; time would tell.

Such calm, such peace enveloped him as the realisation

dawned that Maggie was a part of this; a movement within the music.

※

When he arrived home, he saw that Maggie had phoned; he must return the call. He would light the fire; shower; eat something; relax and phone her. He lit the fire.

The phone rang. It was the call that prompted him to go to Maggie.

※

Hastily, Sentinel showered, changed, threw together a few things; grabbed a snack and something to drink; headed out to the car.

He drove keeping his destination in mind. Was he wrong? He did not think so. Maggie needed him and would not say. It was in her nature to deny herself respite; forgive herself. Yet, she had nothing to forgive, as far as Sentinel could sense.

Her beauty stretched before him as he drove. He loved every part of her and hoped that she would not withdraw from him a second time. The night wore on.

Eventually signs of dawn appeared; the sky took on a fresh light. Sentinel was not far off.

A little nearer, he would pull in to check the address in case he needed to ask an early worker for directions.

As it happened, he stopped outside a newsagent's, brightly lit at the corner of a barely lit street. He went in and asked; Maggie was only a few turns away. Sentinel pressed on.

He arrived at the block of flats and rang a bell; Maggie's. No answer. He tried again. The main door opened and a man stepped out.

"Looking for someone?" he asked.

Sentinel showed him the address with Maggie's name, that he had scribbled at the top.

"Second floor," said the man, holding the door so that Sentinel could enter.

"Thanks," answered Sentinel.

He made for the stairs, bounding up, anxious to get to Maggie's door. He rang. No answer. Rang again. The door opposite opened and a woman appeared.

"She's not there," she told Sentinel and explained the situation; gave him the address of a hospice. Bewildered and in shock, Sentinel started down the stairs.

"There's a lift!" the woman called, but he was already out of sight.

"Maggie." All he could think was her name, which he repeated over and over in his mind.

Sentinel arrived unaware of how he had driven there. Once more, he stood at the entrance to a building. He rang; was ushered in when he spoke Maggie's name; was guided to a small room in which Maggie lay.

"There has been a rapid decline," he was told. "It was too far on when Maggie sought help."

He stood in the doorway; watched her sleep; moved across to a chair by the bed and sat, gazing at her face; its frailty and its grace. Sentinel found Maggie's hand; stroked it gently; waited.

Her beauty generated notes of music within his mind; some barely discernible; almost incomplete. Sentinel collected them to add to the music he had experienced in the tent and which played in the recess of his mind.

※

Maggie opened her eyes; saw Sentinel.
"Sentinel," she smiled. "It *is* you."
"It's me," he replied. "I came."
"Thank you."
"My pleasure," he, in turn, smiled; leaned forward and kissed her forehead. She put her arms around him, but had not strength to hug.
"Stay with me," she urged.
"Shh. Don't worry. I am not going anywhere without you."
Maggie released her arms; gazed at Sentinel.
A while later, she spoke again.
"Sentinel."
"Yes, Maggie."
Their names filled the small space that was the room.
"Sentinel. Take me with you. To the bungalow."
"I don't …." Her words stunned Sentinel.
"Please. I need to be there."
He gathered his thoughts; his senses. Realised.

"*We* need to be there," he told Maggie and wondered how it would be achieved.

"Now," she added and lapsed into a doze, exhausted.

He knew, then, that this was to be their time; the bungalow their place. He left the room to demand the possibility become actuality.

'It would be difficult, but yes, possible,' he was told. 'She does not have long,' they had added. The words spiralled in his brain.

※

Two hours later, everything was in place; the car made comfortable for Maggie; medication provided and extra given for the journey.

Maggie woke again.

"Sentinel. I am a thief. I have stolen our time. I shouldn't have left you."

"What do you mean?"

"I was told that I was a thief … as a child … but it was not true. It's true now, Sentinel. That is what I am … a thief."

Maggie was distraught. He was distraught within.

"Maggie." he lifted and cradled her, ready for the car. "Maggie, you are not a thief. You gave me time. You were generous."

"Was I?"

"Yes. Know this, Maggie. You are not a thief. You were never a thief. A special person … different … confused … but never a thief. Maggie, our time is to come."

Maggie relaxed in his arms.

"Thank you … Sentinel."

"Now, let's go home. Ready?"

"Yes."

Sentinel carried her gently to the car.

※

Chapter Thirty Nine

Maggie and Sentinel

The day is relentless in its semi darkness. Sentinel drives on; rain hammers the windscreen. He cannot, will not, stop. He must return Maggie to their environment; honour her wish; her desire.

Mid afternoon, the rain ceases its onslaught. The density of gathering clouds carrying the probability of snow lower the sky.

Evening approaches. The distance weighs on Sentinel. It seems as if the road takes them to the end of the earth; perhaps it does. He dare not look back, wonder how Maggie is; alive or dead. There is no sound from her. He hopes that she is asleep.

❈

Eventually, the bungalow is in sight. Sentinel slows down the car; turns into the drive. The car comes to a halt at the door. Quickly, he leaves the car, grasping his keys. He unlocks the door, strides across the room and switches on a small lamp on a side table beside the couch. Glancing towards the grate, he sees that the fire is set; ready to be lit. He hesitates in momentary indecision. "Maggie is warmer where she is until the fire is lit," he decides and reaches for matches. The wood is dry; the fire soon blazes.

Sentinel steps back out into the cold and opens the rear side door. Maggie is awake. He exhales in relief that she has made the journey. She smiles.

"Home," she whispers.

Sentinel lifts her up, holds her to him; carries her indoors, kicking the bungalow door shut with his heel. Gently, he lays Maggie on the couch; brings a light blanket and pillows to keep her warm and comfortable. He kneels on the floor close to her; their faces turn to each other. He strokes her hair.

Time passes.

Maggie leans her head nearer to Sentinel's. Her eyes smile into his, overriding the pain which lies beneath.

"Sentinel."

Maggie voices his name with difficulty.

"I was ……. yours ……. always ……. but I ….. couldn't tell ……. you …… Sentinel"

Maggie whispers his name, a faint smile on her face and, worn with the effort, lapses into sleep.

Sentinel remains at her side, his head touching hers.

※

Aware of discomfort, Sentinel realises that he has dozed. The dying embers of the fire give little heat. It is cold. Sentinel pulls the blanket closer to Maggie's form; places his jacket over it; concerned for her warmth.

Maggie wakes; fixes her eyes on Sentinel; unwilling to take her gaze from him. Sentinel moves to the window to draw the curtains; looks out.

Softly, silently, snowflakes land on the window pane; pure, white, incredible symmetry created for a brief moment in time. Such peace.

He does not draw the curtains; instead, returns to the couch. Maggie's eyes remain open. Sentinel manoeuvres the couch across the room to the window. He raises Maggie, to cradle her, again. They sit as one; watch the snowflakes fall; devastatingly beautiful. The glow from the massed flakes, pure light.

Time is suspended.

Sentinel averts his gaze to Maggie. He hears her soft sigh. Maggie is gone.

'Some day a door will surely open and expose the glittering central mechanism of the world in its beauty and simplicity.'

John Archibald Wheeler

Chapter Forty

Sounding together

    The time is perfect; all motion suspends. The symphony begins; created on the speck of dust that was Segment.

    One speck; one crystal note arises from a droplet in the cold of night to release, as the flake of snow forms, a symphony that soars harmonious; one perfect moment in time and motion; in that instant.

'Snowflake Symphony'

Acknowledgements / Permissions

For quotes used in chapter headings:

Emily Dickinson – Chs 6, 20 – quotes from the poems 'Choice' p61, and 'Hope:1' p16 – Wordsworth Poetry Library 'The Works of Emily Dickinson'

Andrew Duhon – Chs 32, 33 – words from his song 'The Moorings' taken from his album 'The Moorings'

Shan Gao – Chs 1,3,9,16,31 quotes from 'Understanding Quantum Physics' - eBook

Claudia Masin – Ch 36 – poem 'Niños Del Cielos' from her book 'La Vista' - Colección Visor de Poesia, p9

Sir Isaac Newton - Ch 12, 23 – quotes from Sir Isaac Newton - website www.todayinsci.com

Christina Rossetti – Ch 20 – quote from 'Who has seen the wind?' p127 - 'A New Treasury of Poetry' compiled by Neil Philips – Blackie 1990

John Archibald Wheeler – Chs 26, 40 – quotes – Misner, Charles W., Kip S. Thorne, and John Archibald Wheeler. *Gravitation* New York: W. H. Freeman, 1973. (p. 1197 , Ch 40 quote) - jawarchive.wordpress.com

Made in the USA
Charleston, SC
09 September 2014